Finding Love in the Sweet Life:

A Missing Ingredient Romance Novel

By Diann Dean

Copyright by Diann Dean

Please visit www.DiannDean.com to learn more and to be the first to know about her next romance novels.

Dedication

This book is dedicated to my mother. She is both the sweetest and strongest lady that I know!

Chapter 1

If not for all the puking, Emily would have made it to the reception on time. Knowing she tended to run late, she'd planned for someone to cover closing the bakery and left plenty of time to dress, fix her hair, put on makeup and pick up Robin. She'd even built in time for Robin to have a last-minute freak out over her outfit or her shoes. She'd neglected, however, to pencil in enough extra time to clean up vomit. As it turned out, that had been a fatal mistake.

Currently, the front seat of her car was covered with a foul substance she had no desire to investigate further, her shoes were unsalvageable and her business partner was giving her an apologetic look in between dry heaves.

Emily looked down and worked to suppress her own gag reflex. If she could ignore the smell, she should be okay. She'd fled the driver's seat when the vomit had started to fly and had walked around to try to help her friend who still sat in the passenger seat looking shaky and miserable. What a mess.

She took in the rapidly dying light. If they left now, they'd still get to the hotel it in time to meet with the contact Robin had spent the past month trying to make, but barring an intervention from a benevolent fairy godmother, that wasn't going to happen. Even if she went by herself, she'd never make it. By the time she got Robin settled, got back home, changed, found transportation that did not smell like vomit and drove herself to the city, the reception would be over. For now, she would have to just deal with the situation at hand.

Emily sighed, "Are you okay?"

Robin nodded, but Emily noted that her friend didn't seem to want to risk speaking. Given the way Robin had been going for the past few weeks, she was probably afraid she'd puke again. Emily feared Robin might be right, so she moved out of direct range and hustled her best friend back into the house.

As soon as they were through the front door of the small suburban home Robin shared with her husband, her friend bolted for the master bathroom refusing Emily's offer of assistance. Emily kicked her shoes off on the front mat and trailed behind Robin to make sure she was okay. Also, she didn't want to risk getting vomit on Robin's living room furniture. Poor Robin was having a miserable pregnancy so far.

"I'll get your car cleaned." Robin said as she exited the bathroom wearing a fuzzy pink bathrobe a few minutes later. Her dark brown hair was loosely pulled back from her damp face, and she looked a great deal less green than she had in the car. She still looked pale, though.

Emily nodded, fervently wishing she could also strip out of her dress. Maybe, Robin would lend her some old clothes or at least some flip flops since the only place her disgusting shoes were going was the trash. "Okay. It's a shame we have to miss this one, but I'm sure we can set up ..."

"Oh God." Robin cried, her face paling even more. "We have to go now. We cannot miss this." she sounded close to tears. Emily wasn't sure if the tears were due more to pregnancy hormones or to the dismal state of their bakery's finances, which were, admittedly, horrendous. Their bakery had a great reputation and not enough customers to support it. They were too out of the way for their specialized niche, and even their fanatically loyal base didn't give them enough business to maintain their offerings. They were going to have to find an investor to give them the money to revamp their operation or find a new market that they could actually serve with their current facilities.

"Rob, there's no way we can make it now. I can't take my car, and I don't think you puking all over anyone is going to get us a cookbook offer or impress a potential business partner." She felt guilty for being so blunt, but if she didn't lay the situation out in stark lines, Robin would keep obsessing.

Robin glared at Emily and made a sound that was equal parts embarrassed and annoyed.

Emily continued, "Greg has your car, and I'd have to go home and try to find something else in my closet that works." She gestured to her black cocktail dress. "This probably does not smell reception ready."

She forced a calm expression while inside she was starting to panic a little. She had never had much hope for this reception yielding a deal, but they were at the point where every new opportunity was too valuable to ignore. Their opportunities were dwindling, and Robin had really pushed her connections to get them invited to tonight's reception for Selena Grubor, the host of a wildly successful cooking competition show. The two were supposed to chat with the vice president of Indulgence, a prominent luxury company interested in entering specialty diet market, and it was not the kind of opportunity they were likely to get again.

For a minute, Emily thought Robin was actually going to cry, but Robin's face suddenly set in an expression that Emily had learned meant business, "No, you'll wear something of mine, and Greg can take you on the way to his meeting."

Emily protested, but Robin rolled over objections. Emily felt sick. She hated receptions and networking, and she wasn't very good at schmoozing clients and investors. Robin, however, was right. Any chance was better than no chance, and since Robin, who was better at mingling and marketing was not up to fighting trim, Emily needed to step up and get it done if they wanted to save their business.

Two hours later, Emily was considering the morality of plotting revenge on your miserable, pregnant best friend. She tugged at the hem of the silver lace sheath dress Robin had somehow talked her into wearing. On Robin, the dress was loose and conservative. On Emily, it was not. Though Robin had assured her it looked appropriate for the reception, Emily was doubtful. Robin was a small size 4. Emily was usually a size 6, so getting into Rob's dress had required foundation garments and luck. To make matters worse, the strappy matching shoes were higher than anything Emily had ever owned, not to mention that Emily was not the most graceful person under the best of conditions. Her only hope of remaining upright all night was to walk as little as possible.

And now, it looked like the puke, the constricting dress and the awful heels had all been for nothing.

Emily looked around the emptying reception room and fought the urge to scream. She recognized some of the people still milling among the appetizer stations and bar from profiles she'd seen in cooking magazines and food blogs. She'd even caught a glimpse of glamorous Selena Grubor, host of "Best in Kitchen" and tonight's guest of honor, but

Michelle Paul, the executive vice president of Indulgence, the woman on whom Robin had pinned her hopes, was long gone. Emily had forced herself to ask pretty much everyone whose eye she'd been able to catch, and after a lot of shrugs, a sous chef who was a friend of a friend had confirmed that Michelle had made her goodbyes and ducked out twenty minutes ago.

Robin, she knew, would make the best of the situation and mingle. She wouldn't be too intimidated by the fancy hotel or the semi-famous faces to strike up a conversation with one of the local chefs and try to find new markets for their goodies, but schmoozing was not Emily's department. She came up with new ingredients and helped develop recipes to suit special dietary needs. If you wanted to find some good ingredients for a gluten-free cake, Emily was your girl. If you wanted to add a gourmet touch to that cake and sell it to the public, you wanted Robin. She was the public face of Sweet Life. Emily was strictly behind the scenes. Unfortunately, Robin was out of commission.

Emily cursed under her breath. It was time to be a big girl and at least try. When she and Robin had started their business, they had made mistakes in location, branding and product offerings that were now preventing them from expanding and causing their bakery to bleed money. If they didn't find an investor or a new market they could actually accommodate with their current facility and staff, they were going to have to shut their doors for good. Robin had always been the one to take the lead with sales and marketing, but if Emily didn't want her business to fail, it looked like she was going to have to learn fast.

Seeing a table with a chef she thought she'd been introduced to a few months ago, she took a deep breath and plastered a smile on her face. As she stepped forward, she felt one of her dratted heels catch on a small groove in the floor. She let a muffled shriek as she fell into a hard chest. Instinctively she grabbed out to steady herself and jostled the arm of her victim spilling his drink all over both of them.

"Oh no." she squeaked, looking down at her borrowed dress in dismay. This night was officially cursed. Of course, she had to knock into a guy holding red wine, and of course, she had to do it in front of some the most influential people in the food community. To top it off, she couldn't mingle with a stained dress, so her odds of drumming up business had gone from small to zero in an instant.

Intending to apologize for tripping over her own cursed heel before fleeing the room, she looked up and just forgot how to do anything other than stare.

She had tripped into the most gorgeous guy in the room. Of course she had. That was pretty much how her luck was running these days.

Even though she was in sky-high heels, he was still several inches taller, and the cut of his obviously expensive gray suit did not hide the fact that he was no stranger to the gym. He had amazing dark blue eyes, a chiseled chin and a mouth that seemed accustomed to smiling. His gorgeous face was framed by slightly wavy hair that couldn't decide if it wanted to be brown or gold and hinted at days spent in the sun. He looked like a surfer playing an executive.

"I'm so sorry," he said, cringing as he looked down at her dress. She hoped his expression was due to the fact that she looked like an extra from the prom scene in "Carrie" rather than the fact that the dress was too tight. "I'll pay for it, of course."

She shook her head, noting that his shirt hadn't fared much better than her dress. She felt her cheeks get hot. "I bashed into you. God, I'm such a klutz. I am so sorry." She ran a hand over her face and took a deep breath to steady herself, "If anyone should pay for anything, it should be me for your shirt. I wasn't paying attention, and I can't do graceful in these stupid shoes." She gestured toward her feet. "They belong in a medieval torture chamber."

He gave a startled laugh. She racked her brain in a vain attempt to identify the man before her. Though she recognized many of the people in the room by sight, she was positive she'd never seen him before because he did not have a face any straight woman with a pulse would forget.

Chapter 2

He wanted her.

Nick Hawkins had learned to trust his instincts and his instincts were screaming at him that the woman standing in front him looking like a guest at a very stylish massacre was for him.

Nick forced himself to act cool, or as cool as a person could act when standing in the middle of a reception populated with some of the most gossipy people on earth covered in wine and staring at a complete stranger like an idiot. She was worth a stare, no doubt. Probably medium height without the heels, she had a curvy body which her dress showed off to perfection. Strands of her dark, gorgeous red hair had escaped the twist she had used to tame it and teased around her face forming an intriguing contrast with her pale skin and drawing attention to her green eyes. He was mesmerized.

"Let's get out of the way" he said snapping himself out of the trance. He set the mostly empty wine glass on a nearby table and put his hand on her arm to guide her from the center of the room.

She looked up at him confused, and then, their prominent location seemed to register. For a minute, she looked like she wanted to bolt, but she seemed to control the urge and then laughed ruefully, "I guess it's too much to hope no one saw that."

"I'm sure we were totally inconspicuous," he lied as he steered her to the door of the reception room and toward the lobby.

Before she could form much of a coherent thought, he had steered her out of the room and to the bathrooms on the far side of the lobby. Because there were closer bathrooms on the other side of the reception room, the ladies room was blessedly empty.

She blinked at herself in the mirror and let out a squeak of horror. It was worse than she'd imagined. Her hair was starting to come undone and forming a frizzy halo around her head. She'd chewed off her lipstick, and the minimal makeup she'd started the night with needed to be reapplied. Those things wouldn't be so bad, though, if she didn't also look like someone fleeing a murder scene. She couldn't quite decide if she looked more murderer or victim, but the effect was disturbing. Robin's silver dress had splotches of red wine down the front. Small drops of wine dripped from the hem, making trails on her bare legs and leaving small puddles on the floor. She had an awful suspicion that she'd left a trail from the reception room to the bathroom.

Emily grabbed a handful of paper towels from the dispenser and did her best to mitigate the disaster. The most she could say about her success was that she was no longer dripping. So much for her bold foray into networking. Once she was as clean as she was going to get with paper towels and tap water, she pulled her phone out of her bag and texted Greg. Luckily, he had only had a brief meeting and had been planning to get caught up on some files until she was ready to leave. He replied almost immediately that he would be there in a few minutes.

For a moment she considered hiding out in the bathroom until Greg arrived, but she told herself she was being ridiculous. Since she was no longer dripping, she could find some quiet corner of the lobby where no one would see her.

Luckily, she wasn't a well-known face in the local food scene, so it was possible no one who had seen her tumbling act had recognized her. Even the hot guy she'd tripped over had been a stranger. At that thought, she groaned. She had ruined his shirt with the wine, and she couldn't in good conscience leave without finding him and offering to pay for it no matter how avidly she wished to tuck her tail and vanish into the night. She was going to have to complete her humiliation by sneaking back into the damn reception.

She pushed through the door, and started toward the reception room noting with embarrassment that she'd been right about the wine trail.

"Wait," a deep voice called from somewhere behind her.

She turned and blinked at the command finding herself face to face with her victim. It looked like she wasn't going to have to track him down in the reception after all.

Finding Love in the Sweet Life

After dropping her at the ladies room, Nick had rushed through his own clean up. It wasn't like he was going back to the reception, and some instinct told him that if he didn't catch her quickly, she was going to try to slink away. He was determined that that wasn't going to happen.

"Oh, hi," she shifted a little nervously on her dangerous-looking heels. "I'm really glad you waited."

He grinned at her, "Yeah?"

She matched the smile, "Yeah. I thought I was going to have to track you back to the reception."

That was a good sign. "And why would you want to do that?"

She cocked her head and gave him a slightly confused look. "After I ruined your shirt," she gestured at the stain on his chest, "I thought I should offer to pay for it."

"Oh," he said a little disappointed. "Don't worry about it."

"Are you sure?" She looked uncomfortable with the subject, and he wanted to put her at ease.

"Yeah, no worries. It gave me an excuse to leave. I was getting bored, and I'd have sacrificed more than a shirt for a good out."

She let out a surprised laugh and visibly relaxed, "Well, I'm glad to have been of help then." She rolled her eyes playfully. "At least my klutziness had some benefit," she made a face and then continued, " my partner is going to kill me for not doing more networking."

"Did you want to go back in and find her?"

"Oh no, she couldn't make it, so it's kind of on me, but there's no help for it," she made an irritated sound. "It's not like I'm making a good impression in this." She gestured down her stained dress, inviting him to look at her body. He suddenly felt too warm in his suit.

He swallowed hard as she turned the full force of a grateful smile on him. "I don't know, you could start a trend and impress your partner."

"She gave him an odd look and laughed lightly. "A trend for wine stains? I somehow don't think that was the direction Robin wanted for our business."

"Who knows? It could be the next big thing, the cronut of the fashion world. You and Robin could ride it to fame and fortune." Her face was so expressive that he could have watched her talk for hours. He suspected she would probably find that creepy rather than endearing. In the back of his head, something about the name Robin seemed familiar, but he dismissed the thought to focus on the woman in front of him.

She laughed again and then wrinkled her nose. "You might be on to something with the stains and cronuts. I somehow don't think either one of those things is going to help our shop."

"I take it you're not a cronut fan then?" he asked. He considered asking about her shop, but he didn't want to talk business with her. All he ever did was talk business anymore.

She shook her head, "Definitely not."

"Too decadent? Too many calories?"

She shot him a scornful look, "Too little taste for too many calories. Well-made ones are worth a try, but if I'm splurging on a treat, that's not even on my list."

"You never want to forget all that and just indulge, seize the moment?" His hand moved reflexively up to his shirt collar just above his heart. He'd made it his goal to seize the moment in his personal and business lives since he was 16 years old and had realized how very short life was.

"It has to be worth it, and those don't fit the bill for me." she said with a secret little smile, and he hoped he wasn't imagining the sudden breathiness of her voice.

"So, something better than a cronut?" he asked.

"Definitely," she said with laughter in her voice. It was a sound that conjured up hot nights and cool sheets. Nick wondered if he could talk her into going home with him tonight. He didn't have any objection of taking her to dinner or doing the date thing, but he'd made a career of being a dessert-first guy, and it had served him well so far.

He smiled at her, and she shook her head as if trying to clear it, but her own smile didn't dim.

"So, do you want to put me out of my misery and get a drink with me?" he gestured in the direction of the hotel bar.

"Since, we're wearing the last one?" she asked with a rueful laugh.

"Well, I thought it might be fun to try something more traditional this time, or if you'd rather, we can get dessert. I'll even forgo the cronuts." He made an effort to keep his eyes on hers though the temptation to let his gaze trail down the wine stain covering her dress to get another long look at her body.

"I'd love to, but I think my ride will be here soon. I texted before attacking you with wine. If you ever want to risk it though..."

She trailed off, her eyes focused on his, and for a moment, he let himself enjoy the sense of connection and anticipation. Things were definitely looking promising.

He took a breath to reply with the expected offer, but the sound of an incoming text message broke whatever had been between them. She jumped at the sound, mumbled an apology and retrieved her phone from the clutch she carried.

"Oh," she said sounding genuinely disappointed. "That's Greg now." Her cheeks flushed a little. "He got out of work more quickly than he expected, and he's waiting outside."

Nick felt strangely deflated at the mention of another man and the way she'd flushed when bringing up this Greg. Guilt? Regret? He sighed. It didn't matter. Hedonist he might be, but he did not get involved with attached women even when they obviously wanted to get involved. Hell, if he'd wanted a fling with an attached woman, he could have had one earlier that evening. The beautiful and engaged Selena Grubor had made that very clear as soon as she'd spotted him at the reception.

He summoned his best professional smile, and instead of asking for her number as he'd intended, he said vaguely, "Some other time. Thanks for the get-out-of-jail-free card and for livening up an otherwise dull night."

She quickly veiled a hurt look, swallowed hard, smiled uncertainly and asked, "Are you sure you won't let me have your shirt cleaned?"

"He shook his head, "No, thanks for the offer. It was nice meeting you..." he trailed off realizing he'd never bothered to learn her name. Apparently, he wasn't as smooth as he thought

"Emily. Emily McCauley." The name sounded familiar and teased at the memory he'd been unable to retrieve earlier when she'd talked about her partner. It was no use. With her in front of him, he couldn't remember where he'd heard it. He was absolutely certain that however he knew of her, he'd never met or seen her before. He'd definitely have remembered that.

"Nice to meet you, Emily." He held out his hand, and she shook it with a small, forced smile. He noted that her hand was cool with soft skin and delicate bones. "Nick Hawkins. Thanks again for a fascinating evening."

"Nice to meet you Nick," she said, and he flattered himself that he heard disappointment in her voice.

Nick bit his tongue to stop from asking for her number despite his reservations. Involved women were nothing but trouble. He made an after-you motion. She gave him a surprised look and then shrugged and let him walk her the few feet to the hotel door, which he held open for her.

"Thank you," she said.

"No problem," he heard himself respond in a voice that was slightly strained. "Enjoy the rest of your night."

With a small smile, she walked through the door and then a few feet to a car waiting at the curb.

His shirt stained and his mood shot, Nick texted the associate he'd come to reception with to tell him that he was headed home. The sooner this disappointing evening ended the better.

Chapter 3

Emily twisted her hair into a ponytail and eyed the stained dress hanging on her closet door. Now that the wine had dried and set, it looked more like evidence from a murder scene than ever. Maybe the cleaner could work some kind of miracle, but she doubted it. She sighed. A designer dress was not in her budget now or any time in the foreseeable future, but she was going to have to find the money somewhere. Robin would tell her not to worry about it, but she'd always feel guilty if she didn't have the dress fixed or replaced.

She shut the closet a little harder than she meant to and heard an aggrieved meow from the direction of her bed. Her cat, Sage, stretched in his nest of blankets, shot her a disgusted feline look and hopped down to find a quieter sleeping place. *Great.* Even the cat had no use for her.

"Wow, I am striking out tonight," she muttered. She pushed the covers back and got into her bed, kicking all but the sheet away in deference to the warm spring night. She shut her eyes but didn't bother to turn out the lamp on her nightstand. No way was she going to be able to sleep yet, but she didn't feel like reading or watching television or getting work done or listening to the host of voicemails her mother had left her.

A few months ago, she would have called Robin to go over the night in detail, game plan their next business step and analyze her missed connection, but Robin's pregnancy had left her nauseous and exhausted. There was no point in wrecking her much-needed night's sleep. Plus, the last thing Robin needed was more stress about their crumbling business.

Truthfully, Emily should have been thinking more about the business, but her traitorous brain kept coming back to the awkward ending of her conversation with Nick Hawkins. She sighed. There was an undeniable attraction despite the fact that she'd doused him with wine. He'd been flirting with her pretty hard, but as soon as she'd dropped him a hint that she was interested in a rain check on that drink he'd asked her for, he'd turned cold and weird. Had he had only been interested in finding a one-night stand? A guy with his looks certainly had plenty of options for those, but it had almost seemed like he'd gotten mad at her. It had been right around the time she got the message from Greg....

She laughed and rolled her eyes as soon as she had that thought. "Idiot," she called herself. Of course, he'd turned cold. He'd thought the guy picking her up was her boyfriend or maybe her husband. She replayed the conversation and felt embarrassed all over again. She'd been flirting back, and when another guy had come to pick her up, he'd gotten the wrong idea about her. The first hot guy who had shown interest in her in longer than she cared to remember thought she was an unmatched klutz who was trying to use him to cheat on her boyfriend. Yup, that was about how her luck had been running lately. And to make it worse, she actually liked him better for not being into hooking up with an attached woman.

She told herself to just forget him. Nick had been seriously hot and seemed to have more than average integrity, but it wasn't like she was likely to run into him again anytime soon. Plus, she had pretty much no time for a man right now anyway. Resolving to get her head back in the game after she got some much needed sleep, she reached over and turned off the light.

"You need to check your voicemail," her mother started talking as soon as Emily picked up the phone. She was in her shared office at the rehab center working on nutritional assessments for some new patients. With the bakery's finances in disarray, she had taken more contract hours at her old job to bring in some money while Robin ran the bakery. Once upon a time, both of them had worked here. Robin had taught a cooking class for some of the patients, and she'd consulted Emily on adapting recipes for those with special dietary needs. That's how the idea for Sweet Life, their specialty bakery, had started.

"Good morning to you too mom," Emily said bracing herself and massaging her temples in an attempt to ward off the headache she could feel brewing. Ever since she'd retired, her mother had made it her business to try to arrange her children's lives. Emily, her uncooperative middle child, was proving to be a special challenge.

Her mom made a dismissive noise but asked her how she was doing. Emily could almost hear the eye roll behind the question. Before Emily even finished her answer, her mom moved on to what she considered essential news. She told Emily about her sister's husband's new job, all of the cute things her niece had been up to, her father's latest home improvement project and her brother's expected promotion. The flood of hometown news made Emily feel strangely both homesick and like a prisoner who had been granted a reprieve. She missed Branchfield and her family, but she preferred her keeping her mother's smothering interest a few thousand miles away.

The pleasantries exhausted, mom moved onto the real reason for this call, "So, did you get the jobs I sent you?"

Emily sighed. "Yes mom, but I don't need a job, and I don't want to come back to Branchfield." Her mother had subscribed to several Internet job boards and set up alerts for dietician jobs. She had taken to sending Emily all openings within 50 miles of her hometown.

"Really, Emily," her mother began the familiar speech. "With your degree, you can work almost anywhere, a good job with benefits, not these part-time things, and you can be close to your family.

Your niece will be in college, and she won't even recognize you."

"Kelsey is three," she reminded her mother.

Her mother ignored her. "Your father was just asking me what you were going to do about retirement, and I just didn't know." She cleared her throat, "Also, Andrew has some concerns about the bakery."

Emily started counting to 100 in her head. It didn't usually do much good when the source of her annoyance was her mother, but she lived in hope. Snapping at her mother on the phone wouldn't help anything, but really, she was not quite 31 with a job and a business, and mom acted like she was ancient and unemployed.

"Mom, don't stress," Emily tried to sound calm and confident. "Drew is exaggerating about the business," she lied. "We have a new deal close to happening." She wasn't exactly sure about the deal. She did know that her older brother, the accountant, should mind his damn business. It wasn't as if he'd seen their books, but he was forever offering predictions of doom via her parents since Emily didn't show sufficient appreciation for his unsolicited advice when he delivered it directly. No doubt, his latest predictions of her imminent failure had prompted mom's latest bout of worry.

She distracted her mom by asking questions about her niece and tried to stay upbeat until she could extract herself from the call. After Emily had left her job and the man everyone had expected her to marry to move to Philadelphia, her parents had been worried, but they'd at least been consoled by the fact that she had a "real job." When she'd announced that she was quitting her safe, full-time job to open a bakery with a local chef, they had thought she'd lost her mind and had made it their mission to guilt, cajole and frighten her back into the safety of mainstream employment, preferably back in her hometown.

She tried to focus on the files in front of her and ignore the very real possibility that she'd soon have to tell her parents that their worst predictions had come true and her exciting new business was bankrupt.

"You must have made a fabulous impression last night." Robin said as soon as Emily walked into her living room. They'd been supposed to meet at the bakery, but Emily had gotten hung up at the center, and Robin had wanted to head home since she was opening tomorrow and had to be back by 5:00 am.

"What?" Emily asked confused as she set down her bag and then settled into the overstuffed chair facing the sofa where Robin, dressed in yoga pants and a bright pink tee, was curled into an almost feline position. "Didn't Greg tell you? Michelle Paul was gone by the time I got there." She'd been puzzled when she got Robin's weirdly exuberant message that she had "exciting news."

Robin made an irritated noise and pushed a dark curl behind her ear. "Not her."

"Oh, God. The wine thing! Are you being sarcastic? What did you hear?" Emily asked. Robin was a bit of a drama queen. She liked drawing out news for maximum impact. Normally, Emily humored her, but after last night's disappointment and this morning's family inquisition, she did not have the patience for this.

"Huh? What are you talking about Em?" Robin asked giving her an exasperated look. "I mean the fact that in all that stuff you told Greg about missing the V.P. and spilling wine all over yourself, you did not tell him you talked to the owner of Indulgence and apparently changed his mind about working with us." Robin shot her a wounded look. "You think you would have told me that you'd met him, but I guess you didn't want to get my hopes up."

"What are you talking about Robin?" she said trying to resist screeching at her best friend and shaking the information out of her.

Nick freaking Hawkins wants to meet with us," Robin was almost vibrating with excitement. "His assistant called this morning. Oh God, Em. This could save us."

"Wait. What? Why?" Emily couldn't get her head around what Robin was trying to tell her. She wanted to, but she was definitely missing something. Why was Nick having his assistant call the bakery, and how was that supposed to save anything but Emily's depressing love life? Also, why did he want to meet with Robin too? Her headache from this morning was coming back with a vengeance. She rubbed her temples.

Robin's eyes widened and she watched Emily expectantly as if waiting for her to catch up. When it became clear that Emily had no idea what she was talking about, Robin sighed and said slowly, as if to a deliberately dense child, "He wants to meet us about doing a new line for Indulgence, his company, the one we were after yesterday, the one I've been trying to get us in with for the past month."

Emily felt a little dizzy. His company? Indulgence was Nick's company. Had she known that? She tried to remember what Robin had told her about Indulgence, but she definitely did not remember the name Nick Hawkins. It certainly hadn't rung any bells when she'd heard it last night. All she remembered was Robin talking about how lucky they were to be able to talk to Michelle Paul. Getting a line with a company like Indulgence had always been a long shot and one Emily had not been keen to pursue. She'd been more focused on chasing other opportunities. This one had been Robin's show. Emily had only been the one to try to land it last night because Robin couldn't reliably refrain from vomiting on people at the moment.

Holy shit. She'd spilled wine on the owner of Indulgence. Not only was Nick Hawkins hot, he was successful and wealthy. His company had had some bad press about calorie counts recently, but among the well-to-do set, Indulgence gift baskets and monthly subscriptions were major status symbols. They offered ingredients, recipes and ready-to-eat items from prominent chefs, talented newcomers and trendy artisan boutiques. You could customize each basket down to wrapping, so they were really personalized and definitely not run-of-the-mill, cookie-cutter gift corporate gifts. It certainly wasn't a company she'd have been interested in if they weren't desperate, but there was no denying it was a big deal in the regional food scene.

"Are you sure?" she asked still feeling like she had stepped into some bizarre alternate reality. She leaned against the back of the chair and rubbed her eyes.

"You must have made some impression too. Michelle made it pretty clear that she didn't think we were big enough to deal with and only agreed to meet because I called in pretty much every favor I was due. I hoped I could change her mind, but I never thought I'd get a meeting with Nick Hawkins himself!"

"Wow." Emily said weakly wondering what on earth had possessed Nick to show interest in their company. It wasn't as if she'd done anything last night to give him the impression that she was a good potential business partner. Well, unless clumsiness was a category he looked for in his business associates. Actually, she was pretty sure his interest in her had been far from businesslike. Unless the recent drought in her love life had completely killed her instincts, she was pretty sure that man had seen her as a potential hook up.

She heard herself make automatic noises of agreement as Robin went on about how they needed to meet to come up with a proposal and how they should really study up on the company. While Robin chattered on excitedly, Emily wondered how she was ever going to be able to face the hotty she'd doused with wine as her new business partner.

Chapter 4

"I'm not sure that Sweet Life is the right fit. If we're going to do the diet thing, we should go with a more established company. I mean Robin Mead had a good reputation when she worked in the city, but she's not exactly a household name, and no one has heard of the partner, Evelyn McCade," Michelle Paul, Nick's vice president told him. The morning light through the large glass windows caught her perfectly styled blonde hair as she took a seat across from his reclaimed wood desk.

"Emily McCauley," he corrected her absently. Michelle had been harping on this since he'd told her he wanted to meet with Emily and Robin about them doing a line of specialty desserts for Indulgence. The market for gluten-free, allergen-free and diet products was huge, and he'd been impressed by the samples from their bakery he'd had sent over this morning.

Last night, he hadn't been able to sleep. He'd been keyed up from his meeting with Emily and second guessing his decision to back away from her. After staring at the ceiling for a while, he'd given up and turned to Google to solve the mystery of why Emily's name had seemed familiar and why he seemed to almost know her partner.

As it turned out, they'd just missed a spot on the short list his team had been putting together of possible creators for Indulgence's newest line. Emily was a dietician and bakery owner, and she and her business partner had a specialty bakery that had a good reputation but was in financial trouble due to early mistakes. He'd also learned that Robin was married to a man named Greg, so there was a very good chance that it had been Robin's husband who had picked up Emily last night rather than her significant other. That had given him hope. The more he'd read, though, the more convinced he'd been that his team had been too quick to dismiss the pair. To his disappointment, considering his rule against mixing business and romance, Sweet Life seemed to be the perfect fit for the new project.

Indulgence had had some bad PR due to consistently higher than reported calorie counts in some of their lines and the very public firing of the person responsible for the misreporting. The company was still profitable, but Nick couldn't afford to let the bad feelings linger. His instincts told him he needed to make some big moves. Adding a new dietician with a reputation for honesty to the team would make a good start. More importantly, though, Sweet Life's products were delicious and would fit in well with the company's other lines. As a bonus, the bakery had started with a great idea but a bad business model, and the owners needed a cash infusion to stay afloat. That gave Nick leverage, and there was nothing Nick liked better in a business deal than leverage,

"I think relative unknowns are a good idea," he told her. "McCauley and Mead have a compelling story, a great reputation and an original and top-notch product line."

Michelle sighed and smoothed a nonexistent wrinkle in her gray pencil skirt. She'd been working with him long enough to know when arguing was pointless. "Are we still going after Michael Taliaferro?" she asked.

He nodded. "Absolutely. That kid is a genius."
After a big win on "Best In Kitchen," Taliaferro was a household name, and Nick knew adding his star to the Indulgence family would bring in a ton of new customers. Michelle had been pushing for just doing one new line, preferably with Taliaferro, but Nick knew that Indulgence needed to give the impression of turning over a new leaf and moving into the future. Two new lines by chefs known for their exacting standards would go a long way toward doing that. Plus, they needed a line headed by a chef or chefs with a wholesome image to balance Michael Taliaferro's edgy one. "They'll make a great pair, the famous wunderkind and the loveable unknowns. It'll give us lots of great PR to bury the calorie stuff. That plus the *mea culpa* we issued and the fact that we fired the person responsible should get us back on track."

"I see it." Michelle said not sounding convinced. "You do remember that Taliaferro is a huge prima donna right? He's going to be a tough sell."

Nick grinned. Tough sells were his specialty, and he didn't intend to lose either the troublesome chef or the hot baker. "Leave that to me."

Finding Love in the Sweet Life

Emily checked her reflection in the mirror. The charcoal suit did not fit as well as it had when she'd bought it, but it was still passable. Maybe, if this deal took off, she could hand in her notice at the center and get back to a regular workout routine. At least her hair was behaving at the moment. The simple twist looked almost elegant and might have half a chance of remaining neat since the humidity today was low for an East Coast spring day. The look was missing something, though. While she liked the pop of color the lilac blouse gave to the gray suit, she still looked too plain. She wanted to appear absolutely businesslike especially after her first meeting with Nick Hawkins, but this deal was also about selling a brand. Maybe, adding a necklace would help.

She opened her small jewelry box. Robin had given her a necklace made by a local artist last Christmas. It was a delicate silver piece with some colorful stones that would give this outfit some more style without being over the top. Seeing a silver chain in the back, she reached for it and flinched when she saw what she'd grabbed by mistake.

The silver chain with the infinity sign charm should have been packed away in a box, but she hadn't

been able to do it, so she'd banished it here. She
held it in her hand, weighing it, feeling the cool
metal against her skin. Almost without thought, she
ran it over her throat, remembering the feeling of it
around her neck where she'd worn it almost every
day of her life for four years. Pete had given it to
her their senior year in college. She could still
remember how shy he'd been when he'd given it to
her, how nervous that she wouldn't get it. "Forever
Em," he'd said. "you and I. When we finish, I'll get
you a real ring, but..." she'd cut him off with a kiss.
Her math-obsessed boyfriend had stumbled into
poetry, and she couldn't imagine a situation when
she'd take it off. She'd tried to give it back to him
with his mother's engagement ring, but he wouldn't
take it.

She missed Pete every day, and every day she was
so glad she hadn't married him. Loving him in the
dorms had been the easiest thing in the world.
Loving him when she'd been living with him while
trying to finish her degree and then her internship
and he couldn't remember to close the refrigerator
let alone do his share of the housework had been
harder. The closer their wedding had gotten, the
clearer her future had been. He'd finish his doctorate
and comfortably fall into the mold of the absent-

minded professor, and she'd become more and more resentful as the details of daily life fell to her, and then, she'd explode. She had been almost grateful when she'd found the emails.

He'd left his email account open one day when she'd been trying to catch up on the bills he never remembered to pay, and before she could close it, something about an interview confirmation had caught her eye. Before she could talk herself out of it, she'd opened the message. Pete had been setting up interviews with departments around the country for postdoc positions. He'd never told her or asked her if she wanted to leave Branchfield or if she could even leave her job. He'd just expected to follow in his wake like his loyal puppy, being his housekeeper and keeping his life running. When'd she'd confronted him, he'd apologized with such a sweet look of confusion that it had almost made her feel guilty for her anger. He'd assured her that he wanted the interviews to be a surprise, and he'd expected her to be excited about the prospect of moving. She shook her head and took a deep breath, blinking back tears of anger and hurt at the memory. He'd never really understood why she'd been so angry. He'd said he was sorry, but he never really got why he should be. She'd left him a month later.

At first, she'd listened to everyone who told her that she needed to forgive him and look forward, but every day, she'd grown more and more resentful, and all of the little careless things he did seemed to be a reflection of the fact that he took her for granted. She had known the resentment would grow and grow until she felt like a monster and hated him almost as much as she hated herself for staying with him. In the end, she'd loved him too much and had too much self-respect to ever let that happen even knowing that neither he nor his or her family would ever really forgive her or understand why she'd had to end it.

When she'd seen that a new cardiac rehabilitation facility was opening in the Philly suburbs and hiring registered dieticians, it had seemed like a sign. She'd move away from Virginia and have a fresh start, and she that's what she'd done. The problem was that while she was great at her job, she'd sucked at making friends. So she got a cat and Sage had been her most frequent dinner companion for months. Then, a friend roped Emily into helping with a pastry class for residents, and there she met Robin who became her closest and dearest friend. And now, the dream that they'd both put all of their money and all of their hopes into was in the hands of a man Emily had all but thrown herself at after dousing him with wine.

She took a deep breath to stop herself from ruining her painstakingly applied mascara. This was no time to break down. She could do this. Today was another fresh start and she was going to show Nick Hawkins that she was not the featherhead he'd met the other night. This was going to be all business.

With a trembling hand, she placed the necklace back on its hook and closed the jewelry box as if she were afraid it would jump back out at her. After reflection, she decided that a necklace was probably not needed today. Really, simple and professional was probably best after all.

"These two are pretty naive about the production thing, but they're better than most new chefs we bring in," Joe Thomas said when he caught Nick in the hall outside his office. Joe would be in charge of working to develop Robin and Emily's product line and get it ready for market, and this was his first big challenge. His predecessor, Mae Hough, had been fired for allowing consistently inaccurate calorie counts to be published for their desserts. While an investigation had not uncovered sufficient proof of deliberate wrongdoing to warrant fines or further investigation, the resultant public relations disaster had set the company back. This new launch had to be perfect. Joe was good, but this was a big test, and he'd been close to Mae, his former boss, so the adjustment period had been tough on him.

"Right. That's the sense I got this morning, but I can see them doing cooking segments, YouTube videos and guest appearances. They both have a marketable look and a great story. It's what needs to go more mainstream and health conscious without losing the luxury feel." Nick said, glad that he had decided to meet with Emily and Robin this morning and send them off with Joe for the tour. They had ironed out most of the details over the phone and email, so there wasn't a lot to hash out on his end, and the two of them had been so overwhelmed that he'd been able to steer the meeting. Considering that even in the accountant outfit she'd had on this morning Emily pushed his buttons and that was a very good thing. He'd managed to keep the whole thing professional. He'd even alluded to their first meeting with a joke about the wine that she'd laughed at politely.

Joe nodded, the overhead light reflecting off his newly shaved head. He was a few inches taller than Nick and a little stockier with olive skin and until today, he'd had a head of black hair that despite the fact that he was in his early thirties, had seemed to recede while you looked at it. The shaved look made him a little more intimidating, but considering that Joe had a baby face, that was not necessarily a bad thing. "I get that. They have some good ideas and are willing to work with us, but they're really committed to keeping the ingredients consistent, so we're going to have some supply issues."

"We can handle it," Nick assured him. "And having a line that fluctuates with availability might add cachet. We can sell it, and after our issues, I'd rather that than the alternative. Everything has to be above board."

"I set Ms. McCauley up with some of our in-house people to talk nutritional content, but she and Ms. Mead have a pretty good system going. Like you thought, it's just a matter of designing some of our baskets and gift plans around what they do and designing a few exclusives."

"Great," Nick told him reaching for the door handle to his office. "Just have the rest of the paperwork sent over to them, and they can have their lawyer look it over and call us with questions. After they sign, we'll do a press announcement and start getting the line together. I want this locked down as quickly as possible."

Joe took a deep breath and said in the voice of a man reluctant to deliver bad news, "There might be a slight snag."

"What snag? I thought we had this pretty much sewn up with the emails and the hours you've spent on the phone with them and all the time the lawyers have spent meeting. We're being more than generous."

"I don't think it's the money or the exposure," Joe said. "And really, they haven't even talked about pulling out. I just get the sense that Ms. McCauley isn't comfortable with the level of control we want over their brand. She's been asking a lot of questions about veto power and who has the final say at each stage."

"They're developing a line for us. We have minimal input into their original bakery despite the investment we're making except insisting that they maintain its reputation, but we have to have final say in the line they're developing it for us. It falls under the Indulgence umbrella."

"Yeah, I think they got that in theory, and Ms. Mead has been concerned but realistic. Ms. McCauley is still pretty stuck on the incident last year and seems worried we're going to tout their reputation for integrity and quality ingredients without backing it up with an end product that delivers what it promises."

Nick sighed. It was reasonable given the bad PR Indulgence had suffered, but he had never skimped on quality, and really, if he'd just wanted window dressing, there were a dozen famous fitness gurus who would have happily added their names to an Indulgence line without being too invested in what that line contained. The whole point of picking unknowns was to get a product they could be proud of while building a new brand.

When he'd started Indulgence, he'd gathered high-end local foods from gourmet shops and shipped them all over the country to discriminating foodies, and in a short time, he'd gone from a one-man operation to a medium-size business that still had a lot of growth potential. The brand was all about little luxuries and discovering new culinary passions, and it had actually grown to the point where it offered exclusive lines from famous chefs and artisans as well as exceptional unknowns. To get an Indulgence line was a huge break for a small local business like Sweet Life, but even before the scandal, he and his people had to do a fair amount of hand holding with the talent who felt their pickles or heirloom vegetables or smoked meats or whatever were their children. If Joe couldn't soothe whatever was wrong with Emily, that meant it was a little more serious than the usual run of nerves. Normally, that would be no problem for Nick, but given his reaction to the lady in question, he wasn't sure how effective he'd be.

He sighed, "I have a call in five, but if they need to talk, bring them up in 15 minutes, and I'll see if I can't figure out how to get it back on track."

Joe gave him a relieved look and nodded. Nick only wished he felt a relieved as Joe looked.

Chapter 5

"I understand your concerns," Nick's tone reminded Emily of the one people usually used with skittish horses. It only served to make her more edgy. The past two weeks had been a whirlwind of emails, phone calls and meetings. So far, the deal seemed like a miracle from heaven, but she just didn't trust it.

When they'd first met with Nick this morning, she'd intended to express her concerns about quality control, but when she'd seen him again in his big impressive office, she'd been struck momentarily dumb and had spent the short meeting concentrating on not making a fool of herself. As they met with the top people throughout the day, her doubts had grown, and none of the reassurances that Joe, their point person at Indulgence or the other employees had given her had helped. Something felt off about this deal. Robin was also hesitant and wanted to talk to the man in charge and have their concerns addressed.

Now, Emily was back in the lion's den and trying not to let his earnest blue eyes override her very sense of something pixilated. "I don't think you do. Everyone has been great here, but I'm concerned this collaboration isn't going to do what either of us want as it currently stands."

She ignored the muffled squeak that came from Robin and avoided looking at her partner. If she ruined this deal, Robin was likely to murder her, and their business would almost certainly fail, but she couldn't just let them risk their names and professional reputations on something that was wrong. She just couldn't shake the thought of how easy it would be for a big company to take advantage of struggling unknowns. If their business went down, they'd be in a bad situation, but if their individual professional reputations were ruined, they'd be in a situation from which they might never fully recover.

"I can assure you that we take quality seriously here. If that's all you're worried about, I can arrange for you to speak with some of the people who've have created lines for us in the past or even arrange an inspection of some of our contracted production facilities. I think you'll find everything exceeds standards." His voice sounded a bit tight but did not lose its soothing tone. His expression begged her to trust him. It also begged her to suck on the bottom lip that looked a little too full for his otherwise masculine face. She was pretty sure that the last part was unintentional, and her reaction to him made her uncomfortable enough to doubt the wisdom of this deal all the more. If Robin's future hadn't been on the line too, she'd have run far and fast.

She nodded. "I appreciate it, and Joe also offered to do that. I guess I just want to make sure that our base, people who depend on getting a product that really works for their health needs, aren't getting lost in the rush to create some kind of image we can't back up." She chose the words carefully, watching his face. She knew she risked offending him and destroying the deal, but this was too important to her to risk, and she even saw Robin nod. Her partner might be more sold on this deal than Emily, but Robin believed in what they were doing as much as she did.

Nick took a deep breath, and Emily braced herself to be told that this wasn't going to work. Instead, he said, "I'm not going to insult your intelligence by telling you that I'm happy to have this held up, but to be honest, your concern makes me even more convinced than ever that this is the right match. The reason we stand out from other companies that do gourmet gifts is that nothing comes out of here that isn't high quality, and that's not just about taste. We had a problem, and absolutely, part of why we want you is PR, but we also want to get and keep those customers that can't order luxury food from most vendors because they have special needs. We want their business, and we want to keep it for the long term." He seemed to focus just on her, and by the time he paused, part of her was ready to agree with anything he said.

"That sounds great, but I'm just concerned that you all have the final say in just about everything." She was determined not to let her stupid hormones override her good sense.

"We can look at that," he said. "But, I can assure you our contracts are better than the industry standard as far as degree of control, especially for relative unknowns. I think you two have a great thing going, and I think we can help each other and make something truly special. I'll tell you what, we're not going to get far going round and round on the same details. Let me set up some of those calls for you and let you look over the papers, and we'll talk again. Maybe, we'll all go to dinner, get out of the office environment and relax." He grinned at her, "I'll even let you throw wine on me again."

She felt her cheeks heat and looked down at her hands, "Thanks, that is a tempting offer." She swallowed hard and met his eyes. That was a mistake. The words got stuck in her throat as he let all the heat and potential that had been between them the other night show on his face for just a minute before the bland, businesslike expression overtook his features again.

Emily tried to remember what she was supposed to be saying, and when it became obvious she had lost it, just nodded dumbly. After what seemed like forever, Robin, who had agreed to let Emily do the talking this time, answered, "I think that sounds like a great plan." Her voice sounded like she was trying hard not to laugh, "The wine spilling is negotiable."

Inwardly, Emily groaned. She was going to have a lot of explaining to do since she'd been vague about how she'd met Nick Hawkins. Robin knew about the wine, but Emily might have just forgotten to mention that the guy she'd spilled it on had been

Nick. Sadly, she'd helped plan Robin's birthday party for tonight, so no excuse for missing it, short of her own unexpected death, was going to fly, and Robin would definitely corner her for the real scoop.

She forced herself to go through the dance of polite farewells despite the out-of-character response she was having to Nick. She really needed to rethink her current celibacy strategy before she let her hormones wreck her professional life.

He was totally screwed. Sitting at his desk and staring absently at the city spread before him, Nick loosened his tie and rubbed the area just under his left collarbone. It was almost as if he could feel the tattoo there burning as if it were new instead of over a decade old. This was crazy. It was a business deal. He should have played hardball. It should have been instinctive for him to do it. The fact was that McCauley and Mead needed Indulgence more than Indulgence needed them. Yeah, the company needed a health-conscious line, but those two unknowns were not the only game in town, and he'd treated them more gently than even the most famous chef he'd ever tried to seduce into working with him. Hell, if he'd let the meeting go on any longer he probably would have agreed to whatever completely unworkable clauses they'd demanded.

He was going soft in the head if not in other regions of his anatomy. Nick groaned and leaned his head against the high leather back of his chair. He'd thought he could be objective. Hell, he dealt with beautiful women all the time, and Emily McCauley was cute but not a traditional beauty. Something about her, though, just worked for him. He'd seen it last night, and this morning it had hit him all over again. The particular combination of wavy red hair, mischievous green eyes, a wickedly curvy body, a quick mind, a changeable face and a sassy demeanor had caught his attention and his imagination. She was a challenge, and Nick loved challenges.

He heard a discreet knock at his door. He sat up straighter and forced himself to say, "Come in."

Michelle strode in. He surveyed her almost objectively. People were always speculating that they were having some kind of secret office fling, but he'd never given it more than a glancing thought, and really, he hadn't been especially tempted to go there. On the surface, Michelle actually had some things in common Emily McCauley. Objectively, Michelle was probably the more classically attractive of the two women. With her blonde hair, cameo complexion and icy eyes, she was undoubtedly beautiful. She also vibrated with the same kind of reserved energy he felt from Emily, but there wasn't that underlying sense of mystery and mischief he got from Emily. Also, he could not picture the poised Michelle ever spilling wine on anyone or babbling to a stranger about her shoes and medieval torture museums.

When she cleared her throat, he forced himself to focus on what she was saying, "Sorry, I was thinking about something."

"Are we ready to announce?" She asked as she perched on the chair across from his desk.

He shook his head and ignored her raised eyebrows. He did not need the reminder that this should have been an easy get, and he didn't want to discuss why it hadn't been with Michelle. Really, he probably should let her handle the Sweet Life deal, but even as he thought it, he knew he was never going to do it.

He shrugged as if the situation bored him, "They're overwhelmed. We'll have it signed in a day or two. Now, let's get ready for the meeting with Tallaferro."

Chapter 6

"It looks like the birthday girl is having a good time, and the little terror is giving her the night off," Mia Trent remarked. Emily turned to face the tall woman next to her and smiled. The first time she'd met Robin's roommate from culinary school she'd been beyond intimidated. Now, Mia was practically family.

Five feet and 10 inches with an Amazon's build, Mia would have stood out in most rooms even if she'd wanted to disappear, but Mia was the farthest thing from a shrinking violet Emily could imagine. Her long dark hair had a candy-apple red streak dyed in the front to add maximum drama when she flicked it over her shoulder or used it to highlight the dark brown eyes she'd played up with dramatic liner. Tonight she was wearing an off-the-shoulder black top, skinny jeans and the absolute most gorgeous knee-high black boots Emily had ever seen. Her lipstick even exactly matched the streak in her hair. The look was as subtle as Mia ever got.

Finding Love in the Sweet Life

Next to her, Emily felt pedestrian in her blue maxi dress, light denim jacket and flip flops.

"Sure does," Emily looked in the direction Mia indicated. Robin was standing under a trellis, which was decorated with twinkling white lights, in the middle of a group laughing about something. A frosted glass with a bright layered drink and a paper umbrella was clutched in her hand.

"I'll admit Mocktails were an inspired idea, but right now, I'd kill for a little tequila or a splash of rum." Mia sipped the icy drink in her own hand.

"At least this year, people will be able to appreciate the taste of more than the first drink or two," Emily countered. Robin's birthday party was, by a tradition, a fancy barbeque with lots of fun, fruity and potent drinks, but this year, her pregnancy had changed the equation a little. Mia had thought they should just go with tradition and do the boozy barbeque anyway. Robin had agreed, but Emily had thought it would be fun to have a nonalcoholic mocktail party with lots of playful drinks so that Robin didn't need to feel like she'd been left out of the fun on her own birthday. Emily and Mia had worked for weeks on hammering out the recipes and

Robin seemed to be enjoying the fruits of their labors.

"Yeah, and really, who doesn't love a little high fructose corn syrup now and again," Mia said with a little too bland an expression.

Emily glared at her, "Hmm... maybe, I should warn Robin. She's really picky about that stuff since she got pregnant."

Mia gave an exaggerated eye roll and laughed softly, "You used to be a lot easier McCauley. Now, you're becoming a sarcastic bitch like the rest of us. I thoroughly approve."

Emily shrugged with a smile. It would embarrass both of them if she showed how amazing that simple declaration made her feel. Since her break up with Pete, she'd been trying to make a new place to fit in and feel at home, and with Robin and her friends, she felt like she'd finally found it.

"I should be mad at you for denying me alcohol when I so sorely need it," Mia said with feigned annoyance.

"And why is that?" Emily asked. "I thought you were a culinary goddess without the cares of the rest of us mortals."

"Well, that is true," Mia agreed with a smile that quickly faded. "But, that pretty boy asshole Michael Taliaferro is in town, and he's been seen with Selena Grubor a lot." She took a swig of her drink and wrinkled her nose, probably missing the bite of alcohol.

"But isn't she engaged to that football player?" Emily asked not understanding why Mia cared who Michael Taliaferro, one of the most entitled people in the cooking world, was possibly screwing.

"Yeah, not that it matters much. I don't really care whether or not they're screwing like rabbits. I care about them talking and him getting an unfair advantage."

"Advantage?" Emily asked. She hadn't known Mia was competing with Taliaferro for anything in particular.

"I have a guest judge thing on "Best in Kitchen" all but lined up for next season. I know for a fact it's the only open one, and I know he's trying to get it"

Mia said. She flicked her red-streaked hair. "It's a booze and food challenge, and he fits almost as well as I do. Plus, Selena has a pretty obvious thing for him. Well, she has a thing for pretty much all hot guys, but Taliaferro has been on the top of her wish list since he was on the show."

"No way they pick someone like that over you Mia," Emily said loyally. Michael Taliaferro had a reputation as someone who was difficult to work with plus, he was infamous for not really caring about ethical issues when sourcing his ingredients. For God's sake, the man had written an entire cookbook of foie gras recipes. If that weren't bad enough, he also had a reputation for refusing to alter dishes in his restaurant even if patrons had allergies or other special needs. He was exactly the kind of arrogant, entitled chef Emily most despised.

"Thanks," Mia said, but she didn't sound convinced. Michael Taliaferro might be a jerk, but he also had name recognition and star power, and he was a past contestant. "Okay, I tell you not to mope, and I start whining. Let's talk about something happier."

Emily wracked her brain and blurted out, "The backyard looks amazing," partly to distract Mia and partly because the yard did indeed look amazing.

Mia's new South Jersey townhouse did not have a huge backyard, but she had optimized what space she had for entertaining with a trellis, plenty of seating, a state-of-the-art barbeque and enough plants to make the yard feel natural. Emily couldn't imagine a better setting for this party given the clear May evening.

Mia barked a laugh, "Thanks. That was totally random and perfect, so I'll go with it. We had fabulous weather tonight too," Mia said then fixed Emily with one of her patented I-mean-business glares, "Now, you and I both need to make a pact to stop moping and enjoy it."

Emily started to protest, but Mia cut her off with a gesture, "You've been moping over here in the corner by yourself for almost an hour. Stop trying to drown your sorrows in fake alcoholic beverages, and go mingle." She gave Emily a conspiratorial smile, "If you need some of the real stuff, you know where I keep the liquor and the emergency dark chocolate stash."

Before Emily could respond, Mia was off to go do more hostess duties. Emily took a swig of her drink. It really was delicious. Mia had a real talent for cocktails, and she and Emily had come up with some cool combinations that used plenty of fresh fruit. She knew that Mia was right. She needed to stop moping. After all, this party had been her idea, and she wanted to enjoy it. Plus, it looked like their business was saved after all, so she had good reason to be happy. She just didn't trust it and couldn't shut off her worries. To make matters worse, Emily normally had a hard time feeling easy in large crowds. Even though this group was comprised mainly of people she knew and with whom she felt comfortable, she was having a hard time not feeling awkward and self-conscious. Apparently, her talk with her mother and the meeting with Nick Hawkins and his people had left her edgy and unsociable.

She took a deep breath and headed over to the group gathered around the birthday girl.

Robin smiled at her as she approached. "Em," she called, "come over here and tell them I am not lying. Nick Hawkins is way hotter in person than in his pictures."

The women around Robin turned to look at her, and she forced a smile. *Fantastic*. She got to be the center of attention and talk about Nick Hawkins.

Maybe she could squeeze in a root canal later to really make this day perfect.

"I guess he's hot if you like the aging surfer boy type," she said with that she hoped was a careless shrug. She heard a few snickers, a snort and more than one sigh of disappointment.

"Told you it was the hormones, Rob," Robin's sister Kate said. "No one is that good looking, but when I was pregnant every halfway decent guy looked like George Clooney. You'd think it would be the opposite because you're already knocked up, but your sex drive just goes crazy"

There were mutters of agreement, and the conversation moved on. Emily nodded and smiled at the right times, but she felt Robin's speculative gaze. She should have just agreed that he was superhot, and moved on. She didn't know what jealous imp had prodded her to play down his appeal, but Robin certainly thought it was significant. She sighed. She was starting to agree with Mia. A little tequila or rum would be welcome right about now.

"So spill," Robin demanded as they sat on her couch the following evening. Emily groaned, but her friend ignored it. Unlike Emily, who knew she looked tired and a little sloppy in her tee and leggings with her hair in a messy ponytail, Robin looked well rested and neat in a pair of simple capris and a v-neck top.

"Come on Rob; there's nothing to tell. Plus, I'm exhausted." She really was. She'd opened the bakery to let Robin rest after that party, and it had been an unusually busy Saturday with a few complicated special orders. Though Noah, the baker Robin had trained, could manage the kitchen with the assistants on hand, and Georgia did a great job up front, they'd both agreed that if at all possible, at least one of them should be on hand at the bakery. That decision also let them cut down on staff costs, an important consideration given the current grim state of the business's finances. With luck, things should soon improve in that department.

"You can sleep all you want later," Robin said and settled herself more comfortably on the sofa, preparing for a good gossip session, "Now, you can tell me what's going on between you and Nick Hawkins."

"Nothing," Emily said. "You know I just met him the other night, and the only other time in my life I was even in the same room with the man, you were there with me."

"Oh my God" Robin said and covered her mouth with her hand, "You totally slept with him."

"What? Have you lost your mind? "Emily gave her friend a death glare. "Jeez Rob. Way to be dramatic. Plus, give me some credit. Do you think I'd have let you walk into a business negotiation with a man I'd slept with without telling you?"

The look Robin gave her was a mix of relief and disappointment. "Okay, yeah, I see that, but something happened. I mean you definitely neglected to mention he was the wine guy. That's not something I'd have forgotten."

She'd known that was coming, "You were stressed and I didn't want you to freak out since obviously, it wasn't a big deal."

"Not a big deal in that it didn't put him off," Robin countered. "It was clearly more than just a run in, though Em. I was in that meeting yesterday too." She used her hand to fan her face. "And it was getting a little hot in there."

Emily rubbed the back of her neck. She could feel the muscles there knotting, "It wasn't a big deal," Emily repeated. At Robin's suspicious look, she added, "There might have been some flirting, and I guess I left out the part where he asked me to get a drink with him."

"Emily," Robin chided, "I can't believe you didn't tell me. First of all, flirting with a hot guy is definitely something you share with your best friend. It's like a girl code. Second, we're putting our business in this guy's hand, so if you're like on the verge of screwing him, I definitely have a right to know." Robin sounded more put out than angry which was about as good as Emily could have hoped.

"It just wasn't anything," she said again and continued before Robin could disagree or add a snarky comment, "Really, we just flirted a tiny bit at a party. I thought for a minute he was going to try to get me to go home with him." Robin was looking at her wide eyed with her mouth open a little in surprise. "But he didn't," she added quickly. "Greg showed up, and Nick backed off. Plus, I didn't even connect the name with Indulgence until the next day because all you and Greg had been talking about was Michelle Paul."

"Wow, just wow," Robin said. "You and Nick Hawkins. That's one I definitely did not see coming. You always like guys you can boss around, and he is definitely not that." She sighed the kind of sigh that was usually prompted by a bite of some type of especially decadent dessert. "But, then, really who wouldn't go for it if given half a chance."

"Robin!" Emily said.

"What?" Robin asked. "I'm pregnant and married not blind or dead."

"Whatever," Emily said shaking her head. "There is no me and Nick Hawkins," Even though that was most definitely true, she hadn't been lying when she'd said she barely knew the man, though the sentence felt like a lie on her tongue.

"That is a damn shame," Robin said.

Emily made a disbelieving noise.

"Oh, don't get me wrong, it's better not get mixed up with someone so important to our business, but you, my friend, need to get laid, and Nick Hawkins is the hottest man I've met in years."

It was Emily's turn to be shocked, "I thought you'd tell me to steer clear for fear of ruining the deal," she finally said.

"Oh, obviously," Robin shrugged. "But it's still a shame, and if you could manage to discreetly jump him after the contracts are signed and without souring the business relationship, I wouldn't judge. I mean Nick Hawkins is prime fantasy material."

"He is," Emily agreed with a small smile, "but I doubt it will be an issue. I'm sure pining over me is the last thing he's doing, so we're safe." She laughed and then sighed. That was no doubt true, but it was also, as Robin had said, a damn shame.

Chapter 7

"So, are you free tomorrow night?" Nick asked. His voice was slightly clipped as if he were already impatient with the topic.

"Tomorrow night?" Emily asked, confused since the contracts were already signed and there was no more need for Nick to woo her and Robin. After their meeting last week, Robin's husband Greg, who handled most of their legal issues, had been able to work out a deal that gave them a bit more control over their own images and name than the boilerplate contract but still allowed Indulgence to make critical production decisions. Nick had stayed out of it for the most part, and Emily had told herself that it was for the best. Greg assured them that the deal was solid, and Emily had been impressed with the other contractors and the production people she'd met.

"Yes, the dinner I promised," he prompted. "I know the lawyers have everything worked out, but I take these partnerships seriously, and I'd like to talk about the launch and some ideas I had for branding."

"Oh, okay. It sounds like it would work for me," Emily said. She was still not sure why he was calling her himself. He had PR people for things like this. She knew because she'd met them. Plus, she and Robin had their own designated point person at Indulgence. "I need to see if Robin can make it," she told him. She put her laptop on the couch next to her, and twisted her hair into a ponytail with the elastic from around her wrist. Apparently, her wonderfully dull night of reviewing cases, working on guest posts and eating Chinese food with her cat was going to take a turn toward the bizarre.

"Oh..." he trailed off as if he hadn't considered her business partner when thinking about this business dinner. Emily tried not to read anything into that. "Of course, I was hoping you both could join me."

"I'll see if she's available," Emily answered feeling equal parts amused, confused and awkward as hell.

"That would be great. You can call my assistant and set it up if that works for you or if you need a different night, we can do that too."

"Sure," Emily said. "I'll do that."

"Great, I'll look forward to seeing you." he said.

"You too," she answered before he disconnected.

"That was odd," she said to the tabby cat staring at her from his perch on the arm of the sofa. The cat cocked his head and considered her for a moment before looking away and beginning to lick his paw. She took a minute to admire the feline capacity for expressing complete disinterest in such an elegant manner.

Emily let her mind go back over the weird conversation she'd just had with Nick. What was up with that? She'd thought his sending subordinates, albeit very high-level subordinates, to deal with their questions while making himself available mainly over the phone and email had spoken volumes. The contracts and the players involved showed he took her and Robin seriously and valued what they could bring to the company, but given their own awkward start, she'd taken his absence as a message to her not to get the wrong idea.

Now, she was confused again. That call had been weird and awkward, like teenagers dancing around scheduling a date rather than like two adults setting up a working dinner. Probably, she was making more of this than she should. After all, she wasn't exactly an expert on what was normal with these kinds of deals. And, to be really honest, her dating life had been so pathetic since she'd broken up with Pete that she was pretty sure she wouldn't be able to identify normal date talk if presented with it.

"That was monumentally stupid," Nick said to himself in disgust. He wasn't sure what the hell was wrong with him lately. Ever since the problem with the calorie counts had leaked to the press he'd been edgy, and something about Emily McCauley amped that edginess way up, which was why he'd decided to stay away from her and let his people do the hands-on work with developing her line. Instead, he'd just asked her to dinner. It was beyond strange. She wasn't even his usual type. Well, he'd always admired curvy redheads, but his typical date was less uptight and more free spirited. Emily seemed to vibrate like a plucked string as if she had trouble sitting still. Normally that would annoy him, but for some reason, he looked at her and saw a challenge he wanted take.

He ran his hand through his hair in irritation. He needed to get his shit together and fast because he'd worked too hard to build this company to destroy it because of some weird existential crisis.

Now, he'd have to get through dinner with her without making a fool of himself or hitting on her. The last thing he needed was any hint of anything that suggested he had an integrity problem, and he couldn't afford to complicate a potentially lucrative business deal with personal baggage. Fortunately, Robin would be there, and what a moron he must have sounded like when Emily had mentioned inviting her. Truth be told he'd forgotten about Robin entirely. He told himself that he was grateful she'd be there to keep everything focused and businesslike. Unfortunately, his sense of disappointment marked him a liar.

He tossed his phone on the coffee table and looked around his apartment feeling closed in despite the open plan and high ceilings. He was sick of apartments. His loft might take up an entire floor of his building, but he still had downstairs neighbors, and everything felt too close and yet too sparse. He'd always loved this space, loved the comfortable, simple furniture, the exposed brick and the natural light, but lately, it, like everything else, irked him. He loosened his shirt collar and scratched the patch of skin under his left collarbone. It was definitely time for a change. The problem was he wasn't exactly sure what he should be changing. Maybe, when these lines were set he'd take a vacation. He'd spend a week or two on a secluded beach somewhere to get himself together, and then, maybe he'd find a new place, a house with no damn shared walls or floors.

For now, he needed to burn off some this unwelcome edginess. He usually had an overactive mind and lots of energy, but normally he could focus. This, whatever this was, was really annoying. He headed for the bedroom to change into workout clothes. Maybe a few hours at the gym would help him get his head back together.

Emily bit into the seared scallop and closed her eyes in bliss. Too many chefs ruined perfectly good scallops with sauces and fancy preparations, but whoever was in charge of the menu at the cute little bistro Nick had chosen knew what he was doing. The seared scallops served on a bed of quinoa and fresh vegetables were to die for. She opened her eyes to find Nick staring at her with a bemused expression on his face. She blushed and shrugged, "These scallops are amazing."

"No kidding," Robin said giving her a significant look.

Emily glared at her best friend and shifted in her seat.

Finding Love in the Sweet Life

"I'm glad you like the food. There are fancier places, but this is closer for you, and the head chef is fanatical about using fresh seafood and local ingredients. The scallops are always a special because they get them from Viking Village on Barnegat Bay." Emily had to look away from him. Nick Hawkins was hot no matter the circumstances, but when he was relaxed, he was devastating. Tonight, dressed in slacks and a blue shirt that set off his eyes with no tie, he looked more like a surfer than ever. To add to that, he apparently cared about locally sourced ingredients, which was one of her pet causes.

"It's great," Robin said. "I'll have to bring Greg. He loves seafood, and we might as well get out now while we can," she patted her growing belly. Hopefully, I'll be able to actually eat it at some point."

"Sorry about that," Nick said gesturing to her plate of pasta and vegetables. "I didn't think when I suggested eating here."

Robin shook her head. "Don't worry about it. My stomach is much better. I just don't want to risk fish right at this point. I'm just happy that bread and pasta seem to be back on the safe list."

"That's a relief," Nick said with a self-deprecating smile that he had to know was a danger to women everywhere. "I haven't been around pregnant women much, and for a minute, I was terrified I'd made a huge mistake. If I do, please tell me."

Emily choked back a laugh and ignored Robin's glare. To Nick's inquisitive look she said, "That's a dangerous request. Holding back isn't exactly Robin's strong suit."

He grinned, and wow that was a sight. "'I'm suitably terrified."

"You should be," she said, and from the way his eyes lost focus for a second, she was pretty sure that hadn't come out the way she'd meant it to. He had that effect on her.

"Good to know. I'll be on guard," he said, and yeah, she was sure he was flirting this time.

Emily ignored the look Robin shot her and sipped her iced tea. She'd declined wine, though a nice crisp white would have been a great compliment to the scallops. She definitely needed a clear head for this. Nick had followed her lead and was drinking ice water.

Finding Love in the Sweet Life

Nick cleared his throat and got down to business, "I'm glad we could get together out of the office. Normally, this is something I'd have done before we got to contracts, but with the PR troubles, I wanted to move fast, and I knew you two were a perfect fit for us. I know you've heard the basic outline for the branding we're doing, but I wanted us to chat a bit before we officially announce the launch."

"We're not doing a press conference or anything are we?" Emily asked feeling uneasy. She knew she'd have to do some publicity stuff, but being the center of attention was not her favorite thing, and everyone at Indulgence had assured her they would keep the craziness to a minimum. Fortunately, Robin was photogenic, charismatic and had no problem with the spotlight. Emily's plan was to let her handle most of that stuff.

He shook his head and sipped his water, "No, we'll just do a press release. For the actual launch, we'll do an event, probably a tasting with some food critics and people in the food community and maybe some smaller pop-up things. I think Joe also talked to you about some YouTube tie-ins." At Emily's nod, he continued, "I know you two have some videos posted for your bakery, but we'll set up something in our channel for tips on how to create indulgent dishes when you have dietary concerns."

"That's perfect. I have some ideas already. Maybe we could do different presentations for different issues and then some recipes and suggestions for modifications," Emily said. She loved talking about nutrition and figuring out how to work with dietary needs. The challenge of it made her happy, and the actual cooking relaxed her.

Nick smiled and leaned toward her. His whole focus seemed to be on her. It was an empowering and unnerving experience, "That sounds perfect. You already know that's why I went after you both so aggressively. The partnership of a pastry chef and a credentialed dietician is a dream for this type of project, and you two have great chemistry. That's going to help sell the videos and the line."

Emily shook her head. "Robin does the videos. We talked about it with Joe, and he was okay with it."

Nick frowned, "I think that's a mistake. If you want Robin to do the cooking demonstrations, that's fine, but you should at least be on camera and talk about the nutrition part. That's a big selling point for the line."

Out of the corner of her eye, she saw Robin go still. Though the restaurant was full, the conversation was muted as Nick had arranged a secluded table in one of the alcoves. She swallowed hard trying not to panic. She thought about arguing but decided to just be honest. "I'm really not comfortable on camera," she said with as much dignity as she could manage.

"Oh," he sounded surprised. "You just seem so confident that I'd assumed you'd be okay with it." He looked thoughtful. "We'll figure something out. At least consider trying short segments, and if it doesn't work, we'll do something else. I think it would be good for our line and for your bakery."

Emily nodded. Robin had been begging her to participate in their videos as more than a script writer and videographer since they'd posted their first one, but the thought of being in a video posted to the world was not one she was comfortable with. She did see his point, however, and probably, since Robin had been uncharacteristically quiet each time they'd met with him, Nick had a right to be confused about the personality dynamics of their partnership. Usually, Robin was the one taking control of the conversation. Emily took a deep breath and nodded. "I'll think about it."

He gave her a crooked grin. "Don't worry. We'll come up with something low key and make sure you're comfortable before we post anything. Just from talking to the two of you and seeing you together, I think the rapport between you will make it pretty effortless."

"Sure, it'll be great," Emily said wishing she meant it.

Robin grinned at her and then at Nick, "Wow. I think the apocalypse must be here."

"Oh, really?" Nick asked looking puzzled.

Emily glared at Robin, but Robin ignored her and went on, "Oh yeah. You just got Emily McCauley to agree to think about appearing on camera. I've been begging, threatening, blackmailing and using my considerable charm to try to get a concession like that out of her for years, and you do it in a night." She flashed a dazzling smile at him. "Either you're a miracle worker or it's one of the harbingers of the end times."

Emily made a disgusted noise and shot Robin a dirty look while Nick gave a laugh. "I do have a reputation for getting what I want," he said. The smile he shot her way made Emily think that maybe, he was talking about something other than getting her to agree to appear in cooking videos.

Chapter 8

Nick sipped his overpriced drink and looked around the trendy Center City bar in distaste. Everyone was trying too hard in their perfect outfits and perfect hair, engaging in suitably jaded banter in a setting that also tried too hard. The bar was a hodgepodge of exposed brick, reclaimed wood, glass and chrome. The lights that had been strategically placed to make everything look edgier and the walls were covered with ironic photo collages and classic ads, all of which featured kids' toys from the 90s. Nick would have preferred a pub or a sports bar, but this wasn't about him, and this was where Michael Taliaferro had wanted to meet.

Unlike Nick, Michael Taliaferro appeared supremely comfortable here. The bad boy of the cooking world was a few years younger than Nick, mid-twenties rather than early thirties, and he was holding court. There was no other way to describe it. From the moment they had walked in, they'd had a steady stream of women making them offers that ranged from discreet to obvious. Every one of them had seen Michael on TV or in the gossip pages and wanted the bragging rights that would come from being seen with him or from actually going home with him. Nick had gotten plenty of offers too, but unlike Michael, he was not amused and had politely but firmly declined each and every one of them.

Now, Michael was whispering the ear of a blonde with a figure that was probably anatomically impossible without a significant amount of surgical intervention. His dark head was bent to hers, and she was giggling at whatever he was saying. Then, he looked up, shot Nick a grin and shrugged, "Jen, I'd love nothing more to than to get to know you better, but Nick and I have some business to discuss first." She shot Nick an annoyed look but became more cheerful when Michael asked her to put her number in his phone. She complied and sauntered back to her friends with a smug expression. Nick tried hard not to roll his eyes.

"Man," Michael said in his trademark drawl as he turned those famous dark green eyes on Nick and ran the back of his hand over his carefully cultivated stubble, "You must be getting old. There are some seriously hot women in here."

"Yeah, well..." Nick said and took another drink. "I didn't think trendy bars like this were your scene either."

"Nah, I like the dives, but a classy guy like you, I thought this would be right up your alley."

Nick snorted. The other man shrugged, "So, you wanna get out of here, find someplace better, get trashed and cause some trouble?"

It was Nick's turn to grin, "Love to, but like you said, I'm getting old, and I have to work tomorrow. So, you gonna end the suspense and stop dicking around? Michelle said you needed reassurances."

Michael laughed. "Oh yeah, but I wanted those reassurances from her." He shot Nick a challenging grin. "Now, you're real pretty and all, but she's more my type."

"You haven't got a chance in hell," Nick told him, suddenly understanding the point of Taliaferro's cat-and-mouse games and why he had insisted on dealing with a lot of the negotiations personally instead of sending his agent. Nick knew that Taliaferro would never believe that Michelle was a completely lost cause for him, but she really was. Michael Taliaferro was a talented chef with a natural instinct for cultivating publicity and a lady-killer smile, but he was nowhere near a match for the icy, competent Michelle.

"Yeah, but it is fun to try," Michael answered unperturbed.

Nick snorted and shook his head, "Your funeral."

Taliaferro grinned at him and shrugged, "I might surprise you. I have hidden talents."

"Hope so," Nick said. The man was definitely talented, but he had more than enough ego to go with his skill. Taliaferro was famous for using basic and exotic ingredients in bizarre ways without sacrificing flavor and for not giving a shit what anyone thought of him or his choices. Some of Nick's people had been concerned that Taliaferro was a loose cannon, and they didn't want to risk the bad publicity that so frequently seemed to follow him. On the other hand, a line with his name would attract many, many customers for Indulgence, so Nick had decided to offset the controversial chef by also adding a more health-conscious line developed by a pair of very stable bakers with impressive credentials and great reputations. He felt a moment of unease at that thought. Emily and Robin might not be thrilled about sharing the spotlight with someone as polarizing as Michael Taliaferro. He was going to have to spring the idea on them very gently.

"You wanted my talents enough to drag your ass out here," Michael could barely keep the laughter out of his voice.

"So, remind me why we needed to meet here again," Nick said. He was pretty sure by now that the kid was just jerking him around to find his buttons. There were times when you had to do some handholding and times when it was useless. His instincts told him this was the latter type of situation.

Michael gave him an unrepentant grin and said, "Really, I just wanted to get the great Nick Hawkins out of the office. My agent will bleed you dry, but if he says it's good, we'll make some sick sauces and dips for those baskets of yours. And then, we'll make lots and lots of money."

God, the guy was annoying, but that was all Nick needed to hear. With Robin and Emily already on board, his plans for rebuilding Indulgence's reputation and increasing its customer base were coming together perfectly. The two lines would balance each other, and it should sailing from here on out.

Maybe, he hadn't lost his golden touch after all.

Emily's chest burned as she came to the end of a particularly evil sprint. She sucked in air, her face hot and her legs tired as she pushed the handles of the elliptical and tried to keep up with the machine's pace. She gratefully noted the decrease in incline and resistance as she headed into a recovery interval. It was actually a beginner workout, but she felt like she was coming to the end of a marathon. She'd been so stressed and busy lately that she'd been putting off getting her workouts in, and she felt it. This morning, though, she'd decided to turn over a new leaf. Instead of hitting her snooze button and rolling over as she had been doing, she'd hauled herself out of bed and to the gym. She'd promised herself that whenever she wasn't opening the bakery, she was going to get up and work out. She was starting to get sluggish, and that was not going to fly.

She felt good. Oh, who was she kidding? She felt miserable because she was out of shape, but for the first time in a while, she was hopeful. Despite her worries, this Indulgence deal really did seem to have the potential to be an amazing opportunity.

Finding Love in the Sweet Life

The meetings she'd set up with past contractors, the contract changes Greg had negotiated and the dinner with Nick and his phone call the next day had sweetened her on the idea.

As she remembered that phone call, she shook her head and felt a grin spread over her face. The day after their dinner, Nick had called her to run a few things from the press release they were working up by her and ask her about some of her recipe ideas. Since he definitely had people to handle those things, she'd only been able to conclude that he wanted to talk to her, and that conclusion had been borne out when the conversation had turned to food preferences after she'd suggested banana chocolate muffins. Apparently, Nick found the combination of bananas and chocolate disgusting. She'd called him a Philistine and then had found herself confessing to a hatred for kale, which he assured her probably voided her diet guru status. They'd shared food stories and talked about their days, and somehow, the conversation had lasted 45 minutes. He was surprisingly easy to talk to, and though she'd given herself a stern talking to about staying professional, she was looking forward to seeing him again.

She took a deep breath, feeling her breathing start to normalize, and then, the next interval started, and there was no room for in her thoughts for anything except the repeated refrain of, "Last one, last on, last one." She just pushed through it and came out sucking air and sweating hard as she entered her cool down. She really just wanted to collapse on the floor in gelatinous panting pile, but she knew she needed to let her heart rate come down gradually. She forced herself to keep moving through the programmed cool down.

"In other news, the two of the food world's resident heartbreakers were turning heads in a trendy Philly nightspot. Is a new partnership in the works?" she heard the host of the gossip spot ask. She turned her head and wrinkled her nose at the choice of such a trashy tabloid show, but instead of turning back away as she'd intended, she moved her head to get a better look as she recognized Michael Taliaferro. There was no denying that the man was hot with those green eyes, dark hair and rumpled air she thought as the host gleefully recounted some of the young chef's more outrageous actions. Poor Mia. This was probably stressing her out even more. Emily hoped she wasn't watching and that no one mentioned it to her.

"His partner in crime last night has been absent from the bar scene for the last couple of months, and word is he wasn't much interested in socializing last night either." The image changed from a photo of Taliaferro to a picture of Nick Hawkins flashing that surfer boy smile at the camera. The bottom dropped out of Emily's stomach, and she had to stop herself from falling as she lost pace. She end the elliptical's program and wiped the machine down as if by rote as she listened to the woman on the television speculate about Michael Taliaferro developing a new line for Indulgence.

"While sources close to Hawkins can confirm a deal is in the works, nothing seems to be finalized yet. Highly placed sources, however, can confirm that Indulgence has contracted to develop a new specialty line with local bakers known for their health-conscious desserts and squeaky clean image." Here, she giggled knowingly, and Emily started to feel faint. "No doubt, shrewd Nick Hawkins hopes to grab a share of Taliaferro's many fans while muting the impact of his antics by introducing something with more of a family-friendly face. All we know for sure is that these two are definitely as delicious pair." The image changed to a shot of Nick and Michael Taliferro sitting a table in a bar deep in conversation.

"Bastard," Emily hissed, most of the charity she'd felt toward Nick evaporating in that moment. He had known this deal was in the works and had kept it from her and Robin, and if there was anything that made Emily crazy, it was the feeling that someone was taking advantage of her. There was no way she was going to stand up and smile and pretend she approved of Michael Taliaferro, and she was damn sure going to make sure Mr. Hawkins was clear on that little fact.

Chapter 9

Nick rubbed his temples and leaned back in his desk chair. Everything had gone from even keel to a minor shit storm in a matter of a few hours.

In and of itself, the gossip piece was extremely tame. It must have been a slow day for them to have even aired it, but then again, it did involve Michael Taliaferro, and Michael Taliaferro was to gossip reporters as honey was to bees. Hell, that was one of his major selling points. The public was interested in him to an almost disturbing degree.

What frightened Nick was that the damn gossip program seemed to have an inside source at Indulgence. The host, Michaela Winters, wasn't exactly a top-notch investigative journalist, but she did have a reputation for cultivating excellent local sources. He just hadn't been aware any of her sources were part of his inner circle. After the calorie-count debacle, they'd really tightened information security at Indulgence, and there weren't many people who knew Nick was close to a deal with Michael Taliaferro. The only people who did know were those Nick trusted implicitly, and one of them had talked to someone.

He sighed. Really, the problem wasn't that bad in the scheme of things. He'd been robbed of the punch of a surprise announcement, but the leak would create buzz and anticipation for the new line. It was mostly a fair trade, but it seemed he'd underestimated how polarizing the choice was going to be especially in the food world. Some of Michael's past stunts, including serving a vegetarian customer bread and water when she demanded accommodation and playing a prank on a customer faking allergies, sat badly with some people, and Nick admitted the man could be an immature asshole. He was, however, a bankable asshole. They were just going to have to work a little harder than he'd expected to downplay some of the kid's rougher edges.

To make matters more complicated, Emily and Robin were not happy that he hadn't told them he had the Taliaferro deal in the works during negotiations. Apparently, they objected to the man's reputation and wanted to stay far away from it. He'd known they might have concerns, but it seemed there was going to be more resistance to a joint launch from that quarter than any of his people had expected.

He picked up the phone and hit Emily's number. From her messages, she was more irate of the two. He'd considered calling Robin instead, but in the long run, it was probably better to tackle the tougher challenge. From what he'd observed of the two of them, he thought that if he could get Emily on his side, she'd talk Robin down, but if he placated Robin, Emily would simply talk her back into a fury at first opportunity.

"Hello," she answered, sounding pissed. She'd obviously been expecting this call. He decided to play it cool and businesslike.

"Hi Emily. I just wanted to touch base about the leak. I know it was a surprise, and I'm sorry you had to find out that way."

Her voice held barely leashed anger, "I don't think there would have been a good way to find that out. It was a pretty big thing to keep from us especially since Michael Taliaferro is pretty much everything you told us you didn't want for this brand."

"We should talk about it. I think once we do, you'll see that we have a plan."

"One that you never bothered to tell us about when you were talking about total transparency." She snorted, "Michael Taliaferro? Really? Could you not get Justin Bieber to do a line for you? He's probably twice as mature. Oh, but then he hasn't built a reputation on animal torture and treating customers like trash."

He flinched. Apparently, she was a little more than just upset. He seemed to have miscalculated.

He tried to sound reassuring, "I think once we talk about it, you'll see how this fits into the vision we've discussed. I didn't want to jump the gun and spring it on you before we had a firm deal with him."

"Vision we've discussed?" she asked suspiciously. "You're not saying you want us to do some kind of joint campaign are you?"

Nick sighed. He wished he could assure her that he didn't, but much of his strategy required joint appearances. "We can discuss that." he said.

Before he could say anymore, she cut him off, "Discuss it? We didn't agree to this. When you talked to us, you assured us that our reputation was a high priority, and being associated with Michael

Taliaferro will damage it in the eyes of our customer base."

Nick knew she had a point. Sweet Life would take a small hit with its existing base. He'd always known that, but he'd reasoned that the growth in business from the increased exposure would mitigate the financial impact. Also, they would benefit from association with a chef of Taliaferro's caliber even if some die-hards thought they'd sold out. He'd honestly believed they'd be better off in the long run. Somehow though, he didn't think that was going to play well with Emily right at this moment.

He took a steadying breath, "The damage, if it even happens, will be minor, and the gains will far outweigh any small losses you incur."

"So, you considered that and decided what was best for us without telling us what was going on?" She sounded more resigned than furious now, "I knew something was off. I should have listened to my gut."

"And what? Let your business go bankrupt instead of taking a sweetheart of a deal? Remember, I looked at your financials before I ever made you an offer, and you did the right thing for your company," he told her, his irritation with the whole situation making him less tactful than he'd intended.

She gave a humorless laugh, "You got us to sign the deal knowing this was in the works, and you never mentioned it. All that stuff you were spouting integrity and honesty was spin. That calorie scandal wasn't some fluke. It was a warning sign, and we ignored it."

He felt as if she'd punched him in the gut because she was right. He'd talked about how important integrity was, and then, he'd deliberately withheld information from her. True, it was all part of staying alive in business, but he felt really shitty about it. Unfortunately, he couldn't afford to back down.

"Look, Emily" he said. "Why don't you and I and Robin sit down. We can figure out something that works for everyone. Maybe, we can minimize any connection," he conceded thinking his plans for some crossover products were probably not going to happen. "We'll do a joint kick off and then the lines can be mostly separate if that's what everyone wants."

They tentatively set a time to meet. She was pissed, and for the first time in a very long time, Nick wasn't sure if he could bring her around to his way of thinking. She was stubborn and the effect she had on him seemed to rob him of most of his easy charm whenever he was anywhere near her.

He shook his head to clear it. He still had another painful call to make. The next one was to Michael Taliaferro whose agent had also expressed displeasure at his client sharing billing with a pair of, "nobody bakers."

Emily tugged impatiently at the hem of her gray skirt. She was waiting for Greg to drop Robin off, so they could go up to their meeting with Nick and Joe together, and Robin was predictably late.

She sighed, trying to take comfort in the fact that even if she felt like crap, she looked pretty good. She'd taken special care with her appearance today knowing she'd need the confidence boost. Her skirt, which was narrowly cut, hit just above the knee and looked hot while still being professional. The medium heels of her black shoes added just enough height to give her confidence without making her feel like she was in danger of fracturing her ankle every time she took a step. Her emerald green top made her feel more vibrant and powerful than the pale, neutral-colored ones she typically chose for business meetings. She'd actually bothered with eye makeup today and had tamed her hair into semi-coherent waves. The contrast of the dark red waves and the green shirt reminded her of Poison Ivy, her favorite Batman villain, and she like the effect. She'd wanted to feel dangerous today, to feel like anything but the kind of woman who had to smile and make the best of things while people treated her like a doormat.

She took a deep breath and tried to relax. She was pretty sure her blood pressure had been dangerously high since she'd heard the news about Michael Taliaferro and Indulgence. Unfortunately, this needed to work both because Sweet Life wouldn't survive if it didn't, and because they already had a contract. Greg had made it very clear to both her and Robin that while what Nick had done was shitty, it wasn't a breach of the letter of their agreement. Even if they could get out of the deal they'd made and somehow keep the shop open, they'd be damaged goods in the eyes of potential investors because everyone would assume Indulgence had cut them loose. No one would believe they'd backed out of such a potentially lucrative deal no matter how they spun it.

Emily looked out the large window that faced the street and tapped her foot in annoyance. She reached into her bag for her phone intending to text

Robin that she had gone up and to meet her up there when a deep drawl sounded behind her.

"It's a damn shame to keep a lady waiting."

She turned around to see the man who was a large part of the reason for her current agitation grinning his lady-killer grin at her. When she didn't grin back at him or immediately swoon at his feet, his grin started to droop around the edges, and he gave her a puzzled look. He seemed on the verge of telling her to smile. If he did that, she was going to kick him in the shin. There was only so much provocation a woman could take.

He apparently had better instincts about women than most men who relied on cheesy pick-up lines and good looks to charm every female they met because instead, he said, "I don't envy him."

She knew better, she really did, but she bit anyway, "Who is that?"

"The man who pissed you off. I mean damn, you're hot angry, but right now darling, I'm afraid for his life."

She burst out laughing. It probably was going to be hell on her makeup, but she couldn't help it. God he was ridiculous.

He laughed somewhat uncertainly, and Emily liked him better for the crack in his facade. Big bad Michael Taliaferro was like a two year old who was so sure he was adorable that he couldn't imagine anyone saying no to him. It was really too funny and she'd been so keyed up that she couldn't resist the release of a good laugh.

"What's so funny? You like planning his demise that much?" he asked.

"What would you say?" she asked, knowing she shouldn't but unable to resist, "If I told you that one of the men who made me so angry was you?"

His eyes went wary, and he gave her a look that suggested he believed he was talking to a crazy woman. He gave a quick look around, probably scoping out his best escape routes in case she turned feral, "Well, at the risk of being rude, I'd have to say that it can't be me because we've never met." He put some push behind the last part. She suspected he'd dealt with more than a few crazy fans who'd imagined relationships with him.

"And yet, I'm still pissed at you," she said. Before he could run away, although that would have been hilarious, she added, "Because the last person I want associated with my brand is the man who is best known for cooking tortured geese and causing mayhem."

"Oh," he said with some relief as he placed her. "You're one of the bakers, Emily McCauley right?"

She nodded, "Good guess."

"You're hotter in person than in your picture on your website. You should fix that. I have a guy...," he trailed off when he noticed her glare and cleared his throat. "Right, well anyway, looks like we're partners." He grinned at her, and if she'd thought the first smile he'd given her was the full-on lady-killer treatment, she'd been dead wrong.

Just for fun, she faked a yawn.

His face fell, but he quickly recovered. His eyes sharpened, and he suddenly said, "You should have coffee with me or drinks since we're going to be partners and all."

Then, she realized her mistake. She'd made herself a challenge, and to a guy like this, who was used to women falling at his feet, a challenge was impossible to resist. She really did know better, but screwing with him would be fun and she needed to have some fun. He was so full of himself and sure she must want to jump him that she couldn't help deflating his ego a bit.

"Thanks, but I think Nick probably has the meetings covered," she said and turned away to hide a smile at his expression. He really was too easy. Where most hot men made her feel self-conscious and tongue tied, and Nick Hawkins had the power to turn her into a babbling idiot, Michael Taliaferro reminded her of an attention-seeking toddler. She couldn't take him seriously at all.

"Why don't we exchange numbers just in case," he said with a confident smile. She wondered if she was getting really old because that smile did nothing for her. He was a gorgeous man, but she couldn't make herself view him as the villain she'd imagined last night or even as the sex symbol his reputation painted. He just seemed like a kid playing Don Juan.

It was on the tip of her tongue to refuse, but some imp made her shrug. He rattled off his number, and she called his phone so he'd have hers.

"I'll talk to you real soon Emily," he said, and she noted that he had most of his swagger back.

She just smiled. She had no intention of meeting him, but having his contact information wasn't a bad idea since it seemed like they were going to be tied together, albeit as minimally as she could manage.

As she was about to text her partner, she saw Robin get out of a car wearing a dark pink maternity dress and black ballet flats. She looked slightly frazzled as she hurried into the building only to stop in mid stride almost as soon as she entered the lobby. Her eyes took on a slightly glazed look, and Emily didn't have to follow her gaze to know that her partner had caught sight of Michael Taliaferro. Emily reckoned he hit most women like an avalanche even though she seemed oddly immune. To Robin's credit, she quickly recovered and headed toward Emily.

"Oh my God. Did you see Michael Taliferro? Wow. I mean I knew he was good looking, but seeing him right there big as life was kind of overwhelming." She stopped to take a breath. "I know he's an ass, but he's definitely eye candy." She shook her head slowly. "Anyway, sorry I'm late."

Before Robin could launch into a long explanation that would only serve to make them later, Emily steered her toward the elevator bank at the rear of the lobby. They had a different good-looking jerk to deal with right now.

Chapter 10

Nick shifted in the leather chair that faced the long couch in the sitting area portion of his office. He did his best to focus on Robin, trying not to look at Emily unless he had to avoid outright rudeness. Normally, he was attracted to her, but today she looked so hot he was having trouble concentrating. As long as he focused on Robin, the meeting seemed to be going better than he'd expected.

Both of them had gotten over their initial fury and seemed resigned to being paired in the media with the culinary world's current *enfant terrible*. There was still a general air of mistrust that he didn't like, but he knew that would take time to dissipate. What bothered him more was the anger he saw in Emily's eyes. Despite his best efforts, he had bonded with her more than he'd intended with that ill-advised phone call and the flirting over dinner, and he regretted hurting her with the situation. This, of course, was why he'd always avoided getting even casually personally involved with people he worked with until now.

After they finished their discussion of exactly how the launch would work, Robin excused herself to go to the restroom, and he lost his buffer. Having no choice, he turned to Emily.

She gave him a frightening smile and asked conversationally, "You do know that he's quite possibly the most ridiculous man alive right?"

Nick blinked at her nonplussed and finally got out, "Who?"

She raised an eyebrow. "Michael Taliaferro."

He cleared his throat. "I didn't know you knew Michael."

She smiled in a way that let him know she'd been saving this information to drop at an opportune moment and shrugged, "I met him in the lobby." She shook her head. "It was pretty absurd. On the plus side, it's hard to hold onto a good hatred for him."

"That's good," Nick said tightly. It should have pleased him that she was warming toward Michael because it made it more likely he would get his product tie-ins, but it pissed him off instead. "Maybe we can set up some kind of sit down with all of us as soon as the details for his line have been finalized."

She shrugged and said, "I gave him my phone number, so maybe we'll even get together before then."

"You did what?" he asked. He tried to seem only mildly interested, "I thought you said he was ridiculous."

"I did, but let's face it, he's also incredibly good looking, so when he asked, I just couldn't resist."

He felt her eyes take in his reaction to that. He tried to give her a blank face and said, "Too bad we're pretty serious about not fraternizing here at Indulgence," he told her.

"Hmmm... well, I guess it's a good thing we're independent contractors," she said flicking her hair back over her shoulder.

"You should be careful with him," he found himself saying before he could stop the words. "You aren't the type to handle a guy like that."

As soon as those words came out of his mouth, he knew he'd made a mistake even before saw the angry light flare in Emily's changeable emerald eyes.

"I think you've already made enough decisions for me, but thanks for the advice," she said with absolutely no sincerity.

He opened his mouth to reply, but before he could say anything, Robin walked back into the room.

As if she hadn't just been baiting him, Emily said in a cool, businesslike tone, "I think this has been a productive meeting, thank you."

He got hold of himself and made the expected polite reply which confirmed their next steps.

As the two women were walking out, Emily said, "Oh, and don't worry about telling Michael, I'll fill him in. He was sweet enough to invite me for coffee."

Before Nick could embarrass himself farther by whatever reply he'd have made to that, she twitched her curvy behind out of his office.

"What are you doing Em?" Robin asked as Emily pulled the car out of the parking garage and prepared to enter Center City traffic.

"Trying to drive home," she said. "We can't go the usual way because of the construction. I swear for all the construction delays we have to put up with, you'd think the roads would be better, but no, the potholes are still crazy."

"That's not what I meant," Robin said refusing to be distracted. "What was that with Nick Hawkins?"

"What?" Emily asked as innocently as she could manage.

Robin snorted. "Uh, when I walked back in from the bathroom, I wasn't sure if I should leave again so you two could do it right there or if I should have made you two retire to separate corners."

"He's an overbearing ass." She shrugged. "It pissed me off when he tried to tell me what to do," Emily admitted. She was only glad Robin hadn't caught more than the tail end of the conversation. She'd be really pissed, and with good reason, if she'd heard what had gone on before she got back. Emily should have kept it more professional, but after Nick had spent the meeting ignoring her and talking only to Robin, she'd been steaming. She had promised herself that she wouldn't let herself be taken for granted and ignored ever again, and she was pissed that this situation was forcing her into that position.

"I get that. You two really do need to get a room, though, or stay away from each other. We need this to work Em."

Emily nodded contritely and made the turn for the bridge.

Robin sighed, "I get that there's something weird between you guys, but we can't afford to lose this," she paused as if trying to frame the next part tactfully. "You were just screwing with him when you said you were going out for coffee with Michael Taliaferro right, or have you changed your mind since you told me about it on the elevator?"

Emily shook her head and said, "I'm not sure." At Robin's gasp, she added, "Not completely. I mean, like I said on the elevator, he did ask me for coffee, and I gave him my number, but I left it up in the air. I'm reconsidering the situation."

"Who are you, and what have you done with my sensible best friend?" Robin asked sounding equal parts awed and appalled.

Emily laughed, "I don't know Rob. I just couldn't resist."

"Well, really, who could? That man is gorgeous, but Em, he's a player, and we have to work with him. Maybe you should be careful there."

Emily snorted, "Not you too. Between your reaction and Nick's I must come off as Rebecca of Sunnybrook Farm." She sighed. "Jeez Rob have faith. He hit on me because he probably hits on every woman between twenty and sixty that he meets. If I'd giggled and looked at him with big star struck eyes, he would have gotten bored, given me some ridiculously extravagant compliment and left without ever thinking about me again."

"So, when you said he flirted with you and gave him your number, I'm guessing you left some stuff out?" Robin sounded annoyed.

Emily sighed. She hadn't had time to fill Robin in on the whole story on the quick ride up, so she'd given her a severely edited version. "I laughed in his face when he tried a cheesy pick-up line on me," she confessed.

Robin choked on sudden laughter, "What?"

"Yeah, I know, so not my usual, but I couldn't help it. Really, the man might be pushing thirty, but he's like a preschooler looking for the toy he can't have."

She shook her head. "We've spent the past day building him up as this devil, and in person, he's like a spoiled kid. It was just all so ridiculous that I couldn't help but laugh. Of course, because he's a man that pricked his pride, so he went after me harder."

"So why go out with him?" Robin asked settling back in her seat.

Emily shrugged and put on her blinker, "We're going to have to work with him, so I thought it might be good to be able to talk to him without involving Indulgence or his agent." She allowed herself a satisfied smile, "I thought I'd probably regret it, but it was so worth it to see the look on Nick's smug face.

"Emily!" Robin chided, clearly uncomfortable with her new role as the sensible half of the pair.

"I know. I'll behave from now on, but you have to admit it was good."

"It was pretty freaking great," Robin conceded. "Even Mia would be proud."

At that Emily groaned, and after a second Robin joined her. Mia was convinced Michael Taliaferro was the devil, and she was going to be so pissed that they were now fraternizing with the enemy.

Out of the corner of her eye, she saw Robin's finger touch her nose in an unmistakable schoolyard gesture, and before she could protest, her friend yelled, "Not it."

"Oh no," Emily said. "You are not sticking me with explaining this crappy situation to her and telling her that Taliaferro is staying in town for a while. You know Mia. She's going to go crazy, and start destroying crap. She was your friend first, so it's only fair that you deal with her.

"You're better at calming her down. Plus, you stirred everything up today, so this can be your punishment," Robin reasoned.

"But she probably won't stab you with her knives since you're pregnant and all," Emily wheedled. "You can play up the pathetic factor."

"Hmph," Robin said. "if you weren't driving me and my baby right now, I'd punch you and let you see pathetic. Plus, I called it fair and square. You get to tell Mia."

"You know that the, 'not it' thing doesn't actually count with adults, right?" Emily asked trying to keep the amusement out of her voice. "I'm pretty sure it stops being valid as soon as you hit puberty."

"The 'not it' counts with everyone," Robin countered in a mom voice she must've been secretly practicing. "I'll have you know that the 'not it' gesture and call have been revered components of the social contract for most of human history."

"Oh yeah, the nose thing is part of an ancient sacred ritual?" she asked swallowing her laughter so she could concentrate on the road.

"Sure, it's a salute to an ancient and unnamed god," Robin answered gamely.

Emily shook her head. "I'm totally looking that up you know."

"It's more something you learn by oral tradition through the wise women in the family," Robin told her. "My family has a large line of wise women."

After all of her recent stress, Emily couldn't think of anything that could have made her happier than taking a minute to laugh with her best friend.

Emily wondered if she could be living out some sort of weird fever-dream fantasy while her body was really lying in a hospital fighting off a devastating infection. That would make about as much sense as her current situation given her more than 30-year track record of relative sensibility.

She rubbed a hand over her face and groaned. She had picked a fight with a man who held the future of her business in his hands, and yeah, she'd tried to make him jealous. Ordinarily, she'd have pegged Nick Hawkins as way out of her league, and it would have never even occurred to her that she had the power to make him jealous. There was something about him or the recent roller coaster of her life or the fact that her best friend was about to have a baby or the alignment of the planets. She felt stripped of all sense of reason and good judgement.

She kicked off her shoes, threw herself on her couch, not caring that she was crumpling her skirt, and sighed. Reaching up, she unclipped that barrette that held her hair back from her face and massaged her scalp. She dropped the clip and let it clatter to the table. Probably, she should put it away, change out of her clothes and put her shoes in the closet, but she wasn't exactly on the responsible train today. She didn't have the energy to do more than wallow right this second.

Maybe, just maybe, she could explain away her behavior toward Nick as weird chemistry, hormones and a heretofore undiscovered self-destructive streak. What really had her suspecting she was actually stuck in some bizarre alternate reality, though, was the fact that as soon as she'd gotten to her apartment after dropping Robin at home, she'd called Michael Taliaferro, a man she detested the very idea of, and asked him out for coffee. And instead of acting like she was a lunatic, the frequent tabloid poster boy and bad-boy chef extraordinaire, had agreed readily. He'd even tried to coax her into making it drinks. She'd suspected, though, from his cheerful acceptance of her rejection of that plan, that the offer had been some kind of test. Probably, if she'd let him dictate the terms, he'd have come up with a reason to back out of the meeting. What was she thinking?

Nick had just made her so damn mad with his dictatorial behavior. Was she and Michael Taliaferro almost laughably mismatched? Of course they were, but somehow it was insulting for him to imply it. Fueled by her anger and fantasies of how much it would annoy Nick to be defied, she'd managed to gather up enough nerve to ask out a slightly younger man who looked like a movie star and made America's freaking eligible bachelor lists. Actually, now that she considered it, it might be the first time in her life she'd actually asked a guy who was not her boyfriend at the time out at all. She laughed out loud. What a place to start.

She assured herself that this wasn't really a date. It was more of a business meeting with flirting and put downs. She wondered glumly what the dress code was for something like that and if she had anything appropriate to wear. This being Michael Taliaferro, she could very well end up in the tabloids as a bystander to some sort of ridiculous stunt or other. She ran a hand over her face and tried to avoid thinking about her mother's reaction should her problem daughter end up featured in a tabloid.

Chapter 11

"Philistine," Emily said laughing as she picked up her Chai. "I don't think I can be seen in public with a man who hates baseball. I'm pretty sure it's unpatriotic and even unmanly."

Michael sipped his coffee and shook his head. His smile was relaxed and very different from the predatory public version she'd seen at their first meeting. "I didn't say I hated baseball," he clarified. "I said it was kind of boring. I like football."

"That's because you have the attention span of a flea," she said. Searching for a neutral conversation topic, she'd settled on sports and asked him if he'd seen the Philly's disappointing game the night before. When he'd said he hadn't, she'd asked if he was going to see a game at the Bank while he was in town. That's when he'd told her baseball was boring.

She looked around the small coffee shop he'd chosen and had to admit he'd done a good job even though he'd bullied her into coming all the way out to a little place in University City when he could have named any of one of the many options in Center City. It had been a good choice. The place was small and cute with lots of wood, cozy tables and a laid-back atmosphere. Michael claimed the atmosphere was his reason for making her come all the way out here. Emily guessed it had had more to do with the college women milling around, but she did have to admit, she liked the collegiate atmosphere.

He shrugged, "Probably, so what's up with the rabbit food?"

She laughed since he'd made her point for her and then, looked at the remnants of her scone and shot him a questioning look.

"You know, the health food bakery," he clarified.

"It's not a health food bakery. It's a specialty bakery. We make desserts." It was a common misconception. She continued, "I just think everyone deserves to eat good food. Just because you have allergies or diabetes or a heart condition or whatever doesn't mean you don't deserve a treat." He looked unconvinced. She sighed. "Not everybody makes up food allergies to be a pest. You could have killed that man."

Michael had the grace to flush, "He definitely was not allergic to onions. His wife told me so. They played it up for the cameras."

"You said on national television that all people with food allergies were whiners," she countered referring to one of Michael's notorious stunts as a contestant on "Best in Kitchen."

"I was an idiot. I apologized for it. Plus, I didn't really serve the guy onions, so he wasn't in danger. I just told him they were there to see what he'd do, and he faked some kind of attack. There wasn't anything wrong with him."

"It was still insensitive," she sniffed. "Plus, you also said that torture made food more delicious."

"I did not say that," he told her firmly. "That's a rumor. I did say that foie gras was delicious and people had gotten too soft about their food."

"You make it by torturing geese," she said.

He nodded. "Yeah, that sucks. When I picked it for my signature ingredient on the show, I was showing off by using something trendy, but it is really amazing. I actually have shares in a company that's trying to recreate an environment for free-range foie gras," he told her. 'There's this farm in Spain where they just provide lots of high-fat food and let the geese naturally gorge themselves. There's no gavage. Recreating the process here has been attempted before, but it wasn't successful. The guy who's trying it this time really knows geese and he thinks he's worked out the bugs."

Emily looked at him like she'd never seen him, "Why don't people know this?" she asked.

He shrugged, "Some people do, but with the Internet all the worst crap you ever do or say hangs around forever. I was a 23-year old idiot when I did that show. Now, I just give people what they expect."

She eyed him skeptically and took another sip of her tea. Across the cafe, a pair of young women eyed him and whispered to each other giggling. He grinned his big cocky grin and though she couldn't see his face, by their answering giggles, she'd be willing to bet he'd winked at them.

"So, you are a misunderstood saint?" she asked.

He snorted and set down his coffee, "Yup, that's me." He gave her a strange look, "Why the hell am I telling you this shit?"

"I don't know. And I have no idea why I'm in University City having coffee with a man I refused to work with yesterday."

He looked interested. "You refused to work with me?" At her nod, he shrugged. "I refused to work with you too until my agent convinced me it would be good for my image."

She felt a bubble of outrage but tamped it down. She saw him laugh at her and knew he'd caught it anyway. She sighed and sipped her tea.

"You're really not going to sleep with me are you?" he blurted out.

"You're really the man who keeps getting called a heartbreaker in the tabloids?" she asked with exaggerated incredulity. "Do you make these women feel sorry for you, or do you just stick to ones who've had full frontal lobotomies?"

"You're hilarious," he said and sighed. "Why'd you ask me out anyway?"

It was her turn to shrug. "You're so pretty how could I resist?" she asked with a laugh. "Why'd you say yes?"

"At first? Because you turned me down and that pissed me off."

She nodded. That's what she'd thought. "At first?" she asked.

"Yeah, then Hawkins warned me off, and I got pissed, so we're here." He gave her an expectant look. When she didn't offer anything, he prompted, "Your turn."

She gave him a disgruntled look and admitted, "He warned me off too." After a few seconds she joined him in a laugh.

"Well, I was probably curious too," he said when they'd both calmed down. "At first, I threatened to walk if he didn't minimize or get rid of your line."

At her incredulous look, he shrugged and added, "You know, so it wouldn't interfere with my press."

Her sense of annoyance must be going dead because she just rolled her eyes and gestured for him to continue.

"Anyway, he turned me down flat, so maybe I wanted to see exactly what he was risking a pretty sweet partnership for," he shook his head. "SOB even told me that it'd be good for *my* career to do a crossover with you if you could be persuaded to work with me." He gave a look that told her what he thought of that.

She told him what she thought of his arrogance, and he laughed. Something inside her warmed, but it had little to with Michael Taliaferro. Nick had stood up for her. He'd risked a relationship with a chef way more famous and marketable than Emily or Robin, and she wasn't sure why he'd done it. Certainly, it didn't fit the business-first picture of him she'd had since she'd found out he'd kept the information about Michael from her. This new knowledge made her feel like grinning and singing though. She resisted the urge.

They finished their coffee in companionable conversation. He even almost let her bully him into including a low-sodium option in his line of sauces. He did, however, threaten to make her collaborate with him on it if he had to make it. Emily decided that despite her herself, she liked Michael Taliaferro.

"Emily?" she heard the familiar voice as she was about to make her goodbyes, and she felt as if a weight had settled in her stomach. She turned, knowing who she'd see.

"Pete," she said forcing a smile for her former fiancé. Pete looked good. His hair was still a little unkempt, but he'd cut it, so it just brushed the nape of his neck instead of being almost to his shoulders and caught in a messy ponytail as it had been the last time she'd seen it. With his dark brown eyes, olive skin and mass of dark curls, he'd always looked a little like a pirate to her. She'd found the contrast between his pirate looks and absent-minded professor demeanor endearing.

She got up and stepped into his hug. It was harder and lasted a little longer than she would have liked, but she kept her forced smile and said, "I had no idea you were going to be in Philly."

"I'm guest lecturing," he said proudly and launched into some speech about combinatorial problems that made her head hurt. She had flashbacks to many such speeches given while she was trying to do her own work or as a substitute for explaining why the toilet was still broken or the dishes undone or the bills unpaid.

When he paused to take a breath, she cut him off and introduced him to Michael, "Pete, this Michael Taliaferro. Michael, Pete, an old friend."

Pete gave her a hurt look, "More than old friends. We used to be engaged."

Michael paused in the handshake he'd offered Pete, and Emily saw the moment the devil light came into his eyes. Before she could interpret it or stop him, she felt herself hauled against his hard chest and tucked into his side in a theatrically possessive gesture. He brushed a kiss against her temple. She wished she could kick him in the shin.

"Oh really?" he asked as Pete started at them in shock. She thought about pulling away, but that would have just made things more awkward than they already were, so she smiled wanly.

Somehow, she found herself agreeing to get together with Pete while he was still in town. She thought she'd even muttered a convincing, "We'll see," to his suggestion that she bring her new boyfriend, but she wasn't sure since the devil child she'd foolishly befriended had been blowing in her ear at the time. She really was going to have to kill him.

"Check your email." Nick sounded grim as he gave the terse order as soon as she picked up her phone. She was in the process of changing into workout clothes to further her new gym habit. Half dressed, she sat on the edge of the mattress.

"Okay, give me a minute," she said switching the phone to speaker. She opened her email and clicked on his message, which contained a link. She noted it was to a local gossip site that specialized in celebrity sightings, and she groaned inwardly, knowing what she was going to see before she saw the picture. There she was locked in a kiss with Michael Taliaferro. The caption read, "Culinary bad boy Michael Taliaferro getting friendly with a redhead in a popular University City cafe." Based on the angle, the picture must have originated with the gigglers.

"Oh," was all she could manage.

Apparently, that was not what Nick wanted to hear.

"I told you to be careful with Taliaferro," he said. "The last thing we need is bad press."

"Bad press," she said. "It's a picture on a gossip site. It doesn't even show my face."

"Still," he said. "I thought you didn't want to get in bed with Taliaferro professionally. Pictures of you making out with him are definitely going to create more of a link than a joint press conference."

She sighed because he was right, "I know, but as it turns out he's not such a bad guy, and let's face it, he's hot." She considered telling him the truth: the kiss had been Michael's misguided way of helping her with Pete, and she'd torn his head off for it after Pete had left. Really, though, that wasn't any of Nick's business.

It was Nick's turn to say, "Oh."

Remembering what else Michael had told her, she couldn't resist adding, "Yeah, he even suggested we do a crossover product for his line, a low-sodium version of one of his sauces. It's such a clever idea. I think we also might be able to do some allergy-free ones."

"His idea?" Nick asked irritation creeping into his voice.

"Yes," she said innocently. "Maybe, we can make this work. I mean obviously, I still hate his image, but he's almost a good guy once you start talking to him."

Nick made a strangled sound that could have been either agreement or disagreement. He wasn't going to jeopardize the potential crossovers he wanted so badly by claiming credit, but not correcting her was obviously making him nuts She suspected he was grinding his teeth to a fine powder on the other end of the line. It served him right.

"Well..." he said. "Good. That's...great. I'm glad to hear it. I just wanted..."

"Me to be careful about public displays of affection that could jeopardize the business," she said and nearly started laughing at the absurdity of that phrase coming out of her mouth.

"Yeah," he ground out.

"I will be more careful," she agreed and then because she couldn't resist, she added, "Next time we'll get a room."

The noise he made at that was the funniest thing she'd heard in years.

Chapter 12

Emily loved late afternoons and evenings in the bake shop. They did almost all of their baking in the mornings. If she were baking late in the day, she was either doing a custom order of playing with a new recipe, and she was usually alone. While Robin was the trained chef, Emily was a pretty accomplished home baker and had a knack for recipe writing. Robin's gift was to take the basics and make them extraordinary.

Today was Saturday, and they were doing a pretty good business up front, but the back was a haven. She was multi-tasking by putting together a last-minute order for a client whose young son had soy and dairy intolerances and playing around with a quick-bread recipe for gluten-free people who had issues with lectins, like the ones found in her popular gluten-free banana bread.

She breathed in the smell of the dairy-free chocolate cupcakes she had going. As soon as they were done and cooled, she'd ice them with a creamy coconut frosting she'd colored bright blue as requested.

She carefully washed her hands and moved to another part of the shop where she'd set up a gluten-free station. Cross contamination was a big problem, and although they were careful, they still couldn't offer goods for consumers with really severe allergies because running a totally allergen-free kitchen was impractical. Instead, they provided a lot of information about their practices, so customers with issues could make informed decisions.

Before she could get all of her ingredients together, Eloise, one of their shop assistants, poked her head back, "Hey Em," she said. "There's a guy here to see you."

She made an annoyed noise, but they couldn't exactly afford to turn away clients. "Can he wait a few minutes? If I don't get these cupcakes out of the oven, they'll burn, but I can do a quick consult as soon as I get them on the racks."

"It's not a customer," Eloise said with a slightly dazed look in her eyes. "It's Nick Hawkins."

Emily felt her stomach do an odd flip but decided that it was due to sampling too many of her ingredients. She took a deep breath and wiped her hands on her apron. She wished she looked at least a little presentable, but she supposed there was nothing to do about it now. "Send him back."

Nick tapped his foot and looked around the shop. It was cute, a small, simple bakery with a shabby chic feel. The wood floor was worn and the walls had a white-washed finish. There was a fun glass chandelier hanging from the ceiling. Though, the shop seemed mainly to cater to carry-out traffic, there were three wrought iron tables available for customers who might want to sit and enjoy a sweet. The walls had vintage bakery posters alongside informational signs about the processes used to make the various treats on display.

All in all, Emily and Robin had done a pretty good job of making a place that was appealing to their target customers, but their location just sucked. The bakery was located on the main street of River's Edge, a former mill town that was mostly blue collar and lower middle class. The location was cute enough, but the demographic was all wrong for a specialty shop like this. They wouldn't get the foot traffic they needed to keep open. Really, this bakery should be in Center City or an affluent area like Cherry Hill or Haddonfield, where it would be mobbed with foot traffic and lines of customers.

As he was mentally tallying what a move to a better area would cost, the college-aged woman who had greeted him came out from the back and motioned him behind the counter to the door that led to the bake shop itself.

"Emily said to send you on back," she said giving him a small flirtatious smile. He smiled politely at her and went through the door.

In the baking area, he was confronted by yet another version of Emily. He'd seen her flustered and flirtatious in a designer dress, cool and businesslike in a conservative skirt and vengeful in a clingy sweater, but he'd never seen her as a baker. Today, she wore the same Sweet Life black tee that the girl in front had worn, but she had it paired with a pair of black and white drawstring pants and a white apron. Her red hair was bundled up under a black cap with white trim. He knew she was close to his own age, but with no makeup, in that outfit, she looked a lot younger. He grinned at her and was rewarded with a faint blush on her pale cheeks.

"I didn't expect you," she said, and her voice was half apologetic and half annoyed.

Really, he should have called first, but he'd been trying to talk himself out of coming here all day.

He'd thought that if he didn't call, he could change his mind at the last minute. Ever since that angry conversation he'd had with her three days ago, though, he'd had a hard time keeping her off his mind, and he'd wanted to see her again so he could start earning back that trust he'd lost. Nick knew he could have dropped in on one of the meetings she'd had with Joe and some of his other people, but she'd have been on her guard there, and they would have had company. He'd wanted to see her in her natural environment, to see the woman he'd had instant chemistry with instead of the somewhat adversarial business associate she'd become.

"Sorry but I was in the neighborhood," he lied. "And I thought I'd drop in and have a look at my investment." Really, he'd found out her schedule from Joe and driven out here to see her. Admitting that, though, would make him sound desperate or creepy or both.

She gave him an odd look. "I thought you'd toured the shop before making a firm offer."

He could have kicked himself. She was right. He'd toured the place before making a formal offer, but Emily had been at her other job, so Robin and her husband had shown him around. "Oh, I did," he said. "But I wanted a more informal look."

"Okay, well, we're pretty slow today," she confessed. "Things will probably pick up a little before close, but most of our Saturday business is in the mornings and early afternoons unless its Easter weekend."

"That's not a problem," he assured her. He took a deep breath and had to stop himself from sighing in pleasure. "It smells delicious. Do you usually bake so late in the day?" he asked.

"No." She shook her head. "A regular customer was desperate for a special order after she burned the cupcakes for her son's birthday dinner. I was here working on a recipe anyway, so I said I'd do some for her." She gestured to chocolate cupcakes cooling on a wire rack. "I'm actually about to frost them."

"Oh," he said, suddenly uncomfortable. This had been a bad idea. "I won't keep you."

She smiled somewhat sheepishly, "That wasn't a hint for you to leave. You're welcome to stay as long as you don't mind if I work while we talk. I need to get these done. Marilyn will be here in about an hour to pick them up."

"Oh of course, please don't let me interrupt." A sudden memory of her barreling into him popped into his head, and he grinned. "I'll just stay way over here if you don't mind. You already owe me a suit, and I wouldn't want to be responsible for more debt."

She added, "I'm really only a menace when I combine wine and 5-inch heels, so you should be safe. Plus, if anyone owes someone something, you owe Robin a dress. If you hadn't been recklessly holding that red wine, I wouldn't have to find her a new one."

He liked this relaxed version of Emily. He liked watching her economical motions as she turned the plain little cakes into glittery blue fantasies while he tried to tease her into letting him have a taste.

When the cupcakes were iced and boxed, she lifted one that hadn't made it into the carry box and presented it to him with a challenging smile.

"What's the catch?" he asked suspiciously. She hadn't let him near her icing while she was working.

"No catch. This one's just an extra. It's a little lopsided. I iced it for you if you want it." She shrugged like it was no big deal.

He took the cupcake, used his finger to snatch a bit of icing and licked it. As the sweet creamy flavor registered, he sighed in pleasure and heard her breath catch. Good. He didn't want to be the only one dealing with this extremely inconvenient attraction.

"Amazing," he praised. "I mean, I knew you guys made delicious stuff or we wouldn't be in business, but it's hard to believe this doesn't have any cream or milk in it at all. The texture is a little different than I'm used to, but it's so rich, it doesn't matter."

Her smile was open and pleased, "It's mostly coconut oil, coconut milk and sugar. Some people don't like coconut, so that's harder unless they can do soy too. Wyatt, the little boy these are for, though, has had problems with dairy and soy pretty much since he was born. His mom orders lots of sweets from us, so I don't really mind doing a special rush order for her if I can."

He nodded. That was excellent customer service. If this bakery were in a more appropriate area, it could have gone national with the right management. With an Indulgence line, though, that possibility was back on the table. He started to say as much to her when she reached out to swipe some of the icing off his cake.

Everything he'd meant to say was lost in an instant as she moved the icing-covered finger to her lips and slowly sucked the sweet concoction off with an overly innocent expression on her face. When she used her tongue to lick up the last little bit, he nearly whimpered for mercy. Once he'd recovered the power of speech, "No fair. You gave that to me." He was amazed that his voice didn't crack.

"Snooze you lose," she said without remorse. "You weren't eating it fast enough, and I'm hungry." Even though her words were innocent, the slight flush on her cheeks told him it had been a deliberate tease.

Not sure how far he wanted to take this given their business relationship, he focused on eating and made short work of the rest of the cupcake. The cake was just as good as the icing, moist, chocolatey and lighter than he'd expected.

She shot him a mock glare as he polished off the last crumbs. "You didn't even save me any."

He rolled his eyes at her, "You're in a bakery," he reminded her. "I somehow don't think you'll starve."

She leaned against the counter, rolled her head to stretch her neck and laughed lightly, "Yeah, there's that, but I really need to get out of here and eat something other than baked goods. After a while, even the smell of them starts to make me sick from overload."

Nick studied her. She was definitely flirting with him, and he wasn't sure what he wanted to do about it. Well, he knew what he wanted to do, but he wasn't sure it was a good idea. Was she sleeping with Taliaferro, or had it been a one-time thing? He knew that whatever had happened had been partly his fault since he'd all but dared her to date the man. Somehow, the filter between his brain and his mouth didn't always work right around her.

Instead of asking her the question he really wanted an answer to, he asked, "Since I kept you, the least I can do is buy you a slice of pizza. I saw a shop around the corner." Then remembering she was a dietician, he asked, "Do you eat pizza?"

She stifled a laugh, "Too often actually. I eat pretty much everything. I just believe in moderation and being mindful of what you put in your mouth."

He made a strangled sound. Apparently, his brain had returned to middle school. She shook her head and rolled her eyes at him obviously knowing why he was all but snickering.

Before she could say anything else, though, the young woman from the front popped her head back in to tell Emily she had another visitor: Michael Taliaferro.

Suddenly, Nick's good mood evaporated. If that kiss in the coffee shop had just been a one-time thing Taliaferro wouldn't be visiting her days later. It shouldn't matter to him because their business relationship made starting any other kind of relationship a bad idea. Even so, the thought of her with Taliaferro made him feel ill. He told himself his distaste was rooted in concern for his business interests, since Emily and Michael were both important to the future of Indulgence, but he knew that was a lie.

Taliaferro stalked into the bake shop in a clingy charcoal tee and designer jeans looking stubbly and carefully rumpled. Nick avoided rolling his eyes with difficulty.

"Hi baby," he said to Emily sweeping her up in a hug. Nick watched her stiffen and then relax into it. His eyes narrowed. What the hell was between these two?

Chapter 13

"Robin, get here now. I can't do this," Emily hissed into her cell phone. She'd escaped from the testosterone overload in her baking refuge and barricaded herself in the tiny employee bathroom to, "change her clothes." She wondered if maybe one of them would kill the other and solve her problem, but she dismissed the idea. No, with her luck, Pete would show up too for a perfect trifecta.

This morning she'd thought she'd have a quiet afternoon of baking. Then, Nick had shown up and that connection that had always been between them had flared white hot. Because she was apparently insane, she'd flirted with him when she knew better and had every reason in the world to mistrust him. Boy had it been fun though. She wasn't sure if Michael deserved a kiss or a kick for breaking in when he had. Her hormones voted kick, but her brain told her she should be very grateful for the timely interruption.

Since their coffee date earlier in the week, the cooking world's favorite bad boy had pretty much adopted her. He seemed to find her amusing, so he had taken to badgering her to hang out despite the fact that he had open invitations to just about every hot spot in the city. They'd already had coffee again and watched a baseball game, which he'd complained about until she'd told him to shut up or leave since she was still mad at him for the Pete incident.

"It's really feast of famine with you Em. You go from no men on the horizon to three in like a week," Robin responded once Emily had explained her current situation. She could hear the suppressed laughter in Robin's voice. She didn't really blame her friend, but she was currently having a hard time seeing the humor in her predicament.

"Robin, I am going to open your tool box, take your prized knives and show you my new knife-throwing skills," she said tightly.

Robin snorted and then relented. "Em, I would be there if I could, but Greg and I have a dinner with his boss, and I can't skip out. Can't you get rid of one or both of them?"

She thought for a minute. "Not really. I already agreed to dinner with Nick, and Michael invited himself. I guess I could fake a sudden illness, but then, I'm going to have to referee over who will drive me home. Plus, neither one of them will believe me and Michael will ask me embarrassing things just to see what I'll do." She hissed in annoyance, "Stop laughing Robin."

"It's just that this is pretty much the last situation I'd expect you to get yourself into and..." Emily heard rustling and Robin saying something, and then another familiar voice answering.

Fabulous.

She heard more rustling and then Mia's voice came on the line, "It seems like you have too many hot men to choose from Em," she purred. Lucky for you it's my night off, so the cavalry is on the way." Before Emily could say anything, Mia hung up, and Robin let the callback go right to voicemail. Emily made a note to plot some suitable revenge when she wasn't shut in a tiny bathroom.

Great. That was just what this situation didn't need. Adding Mia to the mix was like throwing gasoline on a fire. She was more likely to actually kill

Michael than Nick was, and she'd flirt shamelessly with Nick because she wouldn't be able to help herself. Emily dismissed the sudden pang of jealousy she felt at that thought. So what if Mia was tall, gorgeous and outrageous? It wasn't like she could realistically have Nick anyway, so why shouldn't Mia dazzle him?

She took a deep breath and decided to just go with it. At least with Mia there, she wasn't likely to do anything stupid, and she'd no longer have to worry about being the center of attention.

She shucked off her baking clothes, and changed into the skinny jeans and oversized turquoise t-shirt she'd brought. A glance in the mirror told her that her hair was unsalvageable after being in a cap all day, so she pulled it into a ponytail and freed a few strands to frame her face and soften the look. A little bit of blush and lip gloss made her feel more put together.

Time to face the men.

Fratelli's Pizzeria was a typical small South Jersey family pizza restaurant with plastic covered booths, maps of Italy on the menus and the comforting smell of tomato sauce and garlic in the air. Emily and Robin frequently ordered take out, so the owner knew her by name.

Tonight, she found herself squeezed into a booth next to Michael across from Nick and Mia. There had been some jostling for seats. It seemed that men were incapable of sitting next to one another, and she'd thought letting Mia set next to Michael might be tempting fate a little too much. Dinner was going better than she'd expected, but since she'd expected an apocalypse level catastrophe, that wasn't saying much.

They'd gotten two pies: one with sausage and pepperoni and one with veggies, and Nick had gone to get some beer since the place was BYO. He'd offered to get her some wine, but she'd decided that as tempting as relaxing with a glass or four was, she probably should stay clear headed.

"So," Emily asked Mia, who was glaring at Michael like he was a bug, "How'd you get the night off? I thought you were cooking."

"Yeah, I was supposed to be, but Mark needs to get experience running the kitchen on a weekend, so I got an unexpected night off." She flipped a section of crimson-tipped hair out of her face and glared across the table at Michael as if daring him to say something. He gave her a bored look that seemed to annoy her, but she kept quiet about it.

Emily sighed, and her eyes met Nick's. He smiled at her. She felt warm inside, and before she could help herself, she smiled back.

Mia cleared her throat, and Emily looked away. Surprisingly, Michael steered the conversation into safe territory by asking Mia about her restaurant. She gave him a frosty but polite answer.

Emily opened her mouth to try to keep the safe, polite dinner conversation going, but she sucked in a breath instead as she felt Michael's hand squeeze her knee. Apparently, she'd been too quick to give him credit for being an adult. He'd caught that look between her and Nick and had decided to start trouble.

Nick stiffened across the table, and Mia rolled her eyes. Conscious of her audience and aware Michael had done it because he lived to stir shit up, she put her hand over his and stroked his fingers. He had his eyes half shut like a pleased cat. She wanted to roll her eyes at his overacting, but instead, she dug her nails into the top of his hand. She must not be a very nice person because his pained jump and stifled whimper made her want to grin in triumph. Her point made, Emily pulled her hand back, and Michael's palm left her knee.

They finished their pizza in semi-awkward silence. When the painful meal was finally over, Emily breathed a sigh of relief and reached for her keys only to have Michael snatch them from her hand.

"I'll drive baby. I know you wanted to go out, but I'm thinking another night in sounds like a better plan. We could watch another game." He put so much innuendo on the last word that someone with half a brain would have had no trouble catching his meaning. Emily groaned inwardly. Nick bristled and Mia shot her a disgusted look.

She'd told Mia that Michael was just playing it up for Nick because he'd pissed them both off by trying to warn them off one another, but her look told Emily she was starting to reevaluate the situation.

"Where's your rental?" Emily asked him suspiciously, ignoring the innuendo.

"Back in the city," he said innocently.

She took a deep breath to keep from murdering him on the spot and asked, "How is it in the city when you're here?"

"Oh, I took the train, so I didn't have to mess with it."

"You took the train?" Mia asked surprised. "You mean you took the speed line to the Riverline with all the normal people?"

"I like people," he shrugged. "I always have the best time on the train. Plus, if I want to drink, there's no worry."

"So, you took the train so you wouldn't have to drink and drive, but you want to drive Em's car after a few beers?" Mia asked, not disguising her scorn.

Michael shrugged. Emily was kind of amazed at his ability to let sarcasm and scorn sail right over his head.

Taking the train had been a good idea, but Emily was pretty sure Michael hadn't done it to be responsible. He'd done it so she'd be stuck with him. For a guy who supposedly lived to party, he'd been oddly interested in hanging out and talking and avoiding the spotlight. After their initial coffee date, he hadn't even attempted to flirt with her once when they were alone. Mostly, when he wasn't trying to piss Nick off, he treated her like a cross between an older sister and a buddy.

"I can run you home," Nick sneered sounding as if he were speaking through clenched teeth.

"Thanks." Michael gave Nick a smile. "But Em doesn't mind if I crash. Do you Em?" he asked squeezing her shoulders.

She thought about punching him in the mouth, but instead, she gave him what she hoped was a regretful look. "You know I've got to be up early tomorrow to open. You'll probably be happier back at your hotel."

He opened his mouth, undoubtedly to say something outrageous, but her death glare cut him off. He shrugged, "Sure babe, but I'll see you tomorrow." He kissed her, grinned and then, gave her a quick swat on her butt.

She gave a small yelp and glared at him, but he didn't seem to care. Nick stiffly bid them good night and left with Michael in tow.

"You need to fix that," Mia told her watching the guys leave.

"Fix what?" Emily asked, but she was pretty sure she already knew.

"Your new pet jackass," Mia told her. "Anyone with half a brain could see that you two aren't really attracted to each other, and Taliaferro is a crap actor. Nick's too jealous to see it, though." Mia gave her a chiding look. "The question is why are you're playing along with his crap?"

Emily shifted uncomfortably and then look a deep breath. "Nick warned me off him," she admitted.

Mia grinned. "Payback? Okay, I get that, but I wouldn't let it go on any longer. Oh, don't get me wrong, a little jealousy is good for men, but Taliaferro's an ass, and Nick is going to move on pretty quickly if he thinks you're interested in a jerk like that for more than a night or two."

"Maybe its better that way," Emily said. "At first, yeah, it was a little payback, but now, maybe its self-defense," she admitted. "Nick controls the future of my business right now, so getting involved there can be nothing but trouble. If he thinks I'm sleeping with Michael, there's no danger, and Michael and I have no interest in sleeping with each other, so we're not going to have any issues working together." She shrugged. "It just makes everything neater."

Mia gave her a considering look and then shook her head. "I don't think that's going to work. Honestly, from the looks of things, I give you about two weeks before Hawkins yanks you into a broom closet or a conference room." She laughed. "Or you yank him. And afterwards, he's going to be pretty pissed about your little game with pretty boy."

"Wow Mia," Emily joked with sarcasm. "You should totally write romance."

Unoffended, Mia shrugged. "You keep believing that, but remember, two weeks at most and you two are going at it like rabbits."

Chapter 14

"Son of a bitch," Nick spat out when he realized what Michelle had just emailed him.

It was a link to the same local gossip blog where the pictures of Michael and Emily had appeared, but this was no tame kiss, and it wasn't going to stay on a small local blog.

The first picture showed Taliaferro kissing an unidentifiable woman with long blonde hair in a sexy little red dress. In the second picture, he was cupping the beautiful famous face of Selena Grubor, the engaged host of "Best in Kitchen," the show that had catapulted him to fame. Since Selena's fiancé had just signed a multimillion-dollar contract with The Eagles, this was going to play on the local news nonstop. Plus, given the parties involved, the national tabloids were going to pick this one up for sure.

Emily was going to be devastated.

On the heels of that thought came the realization that this was going to create a press bonanza for Taliaferro's sauce line. Although at the time, he'd been pissed about the pictures with Emily and worried about the future working relationships of the parties involved, Michelle had pointed out that sex was way more interesting to the general public than inaccurate calorie counts. And a sex scandal involving two celebrities of the food world was much bigger than a tame public kiss between two single people.

At this moment, Michelle was, without a doubt, constructing a strategy to take advantage of the attention these pictures would bring. Nick hoped Michelle knew what she was doing. Selena was engaged to a new hometown football hero, and people were not going to be pleased about what looked pretty convincingly like infidelity. This one could backfire locally, but they'd make it up nationally as long as they handled it properly.

Feeling the need to do something, he tried Taliaferro's number, but the asshole wasn't answering. Michelle said she hadn't been able to reach him either.

Despite the fact that the scandal was likely to help his bottom line, Nick would have punched the bastard if he were in front of him. What the hell had Taliaferro been thinking? He'd started an affair with a woman he'd been working with, a woman Nick wanted, and then, he went and practically screwed someone else in a club. Emily deserved much better.

He tried Taliaferro again. Hopefully, the man had had the guts to tell Emily already, but given his track record, Nick thought cooking's bad boy was probably holed up somewhere oblivious to the scandal he'd caused. He'd leave Emily to find out about it from the news or the Internet. Nick couldn't stand for that.

Nick looked at the time. It was almost four. Emily would probably still be at the bakery, Before he could over think it, he grabbed his car keys and was out the door. She was going to find out sooner rather than later. There was no preventing it, and he thought he owed it to her to tell her in person instead of letting her hear it from a stranger.

"Hi," Nick's voice held the tension of someone about to deliver really bad news.

"Hi," Emily responded wondering how something else had managed to go wrong between last night's uncomfortable goodbye and this afternoon. She'd been swamped at the bakery today, and all she wanted from the rest of her Saturday was to watch Netflix and turn her brain off for a while. She was having breakfast with Pete in the morning, and she did not need more drama.

"I stopped by the bakery, but you had already left," he said.

"Oh, did you need something? Are you still around. I can meet you back there." She was puzzled. What was he doing at the bakery again? She knew they'd had a moment, but unless she'd read him really wrong, he was backing off because of their business connection and his belief that she was having some hot and heavy fling with Michael. It was strange for him to leave the city to see her without a good reason and stranger still for him to do it without calling first. She felt a knot form in her stomach. What had happened?

"I wanted," he paused, and she heard him take a breath. "I needed to talk to you, and I thought it would be better in person," he said. "Would you mind if I stopped over for a minute, or if you'd prefer, I could you meet you at the bakery or anywhere else you want. I'm just outside the bakery now so anywhere in the area would be good."

Her vague sense of unease turned to panic. What the hell was going on? Trying to keep her voice calm, she told him he was welcome to come over and made sure he knew where he was going. He told her he'd see her in a few minutes.

She cringed a little as she looked around her apartment. It wasn't a pit, but there were dishes in the sink and a few papers strewn around. Worse than the little bit of clutter was her current outfit. As soon as she'd gotten home, she'd gotten into her most comfortable PJs since she'd expected a night in. She was wearing a tank top with no bra and ratty drawstring pants. Her hair was twisted into a loose bun, and she'd scrubbed the makeup off of her face. As no one had been supposed to see her but her cat, she hadn't been concerned with being presentable.

Deciding that she'd rather him see the dishes in the sink than confront whatever situation he was bringing to her door in her rattiest clothes with her nipples almost on display, she headed for the bedroom. The five to ten minutes it would take him to get here should be just enough time to throw on something socially acceptable, and if she hurried, she might just be able to toss the dishes in the dishwasher before he actually arrived.

By the time she buzzed him up, she was wearing denim capris with a purple tee. Her hair was in a ponytail, and she'd used CC cream, blush and concealer to make her face look less drawn. He'd just have to deal with the dirty dishes. As his knock sounded on the door, she tried to prepare herself for whatever freaky crap the world was going to throw at her next.

Casual suited her Nick thought as Emily answered the door. She gave him a nervous smile and invited him in. Her apartment was on the small side, but it was homey. She had several sets of packed bookshelves, a comfortable-looking neutral couch and a big overstuffed armchair covered with a cheerful red print. There were framed museum posters on the walls. Beyond the living area there was a small kitchen and dining area. It wasn't modern or sleek, but there was also nothing fussy or overdone about it. Normally, he would have called it welcoming, but tonight he felt like a large awkward invader, as if the bad news he'd decided he had to break in person was too large for the small space.

She invited him to sit. He sat on the couch, and she perched on the edge of the chair. He'd declined her offer of a drink, but maybe, that would have made it easier. He was cursing himself for even coming here, but almost as soon as he'd seen the pictures and realized that the selfish idiot she was involved with wasn't going to man up, he'd known what he really needed to do was tell her in person.

"So what's up?" she asked. Her whole posture was stiff.

"Have you talked to Taliaferro today?" he asked barely able to get out the other man's name.

"No, I haven't seen Michael since last night," her eyes widened, and she looked stricken. "Has something happened to him?"

Her concern for the bastard stabbed him in the heart. Nick shook his head while he thought of the painful things he would like to do to Taliaferro for this. It was a long list.

"There's something you should see, and I thought telling you over the phone would be inconsiderate." That had sounded too formal. He ran his hand through his hair before reaching into his bag for his tablet. He called up the gossip site he'd bookmarked and thought about making an excuse and leaving instead of showing it to her and crushing her. If anyone else had asked him for advice in handling this situation, he'd probably have told them to mind their own business. Of course, since she and Taliaferro were his business, maybe he had no choice.

"What is it?" She got up and crossed to sit next to him. The tablet was tilted away from her.

"I'm probably not the one you want showing this to you, but I wanted to make sure you knew, and doing it in person seemed better." He sounded like a teenager.

She made an exasperated noise and reached for the tablet and then gasped as she took in the headline and the accompanying pictures. Normally, he wouldn't have made a big deal over a gossip blog since most of them printed rumors as if they were fact, but these pictures left little doubt about what was going on.

"Dumb ass," she said.

She looked annoyed but not devastated or even pissed. Maybe, it hadn't been serious, but he'd expected her to at least be angry that the man she was sleeping with had gone directly from her to another woman.

"I thought I should probably show you before you saw it on the news," he said as gently as possible. Maybe she was in shock? He had a fair amount of experience with women, but telling a woman that her lover was cheating on her was uncharted territory. He wasn't sure what kind of response was normal in this situation.

She looked confused for a minute and then guilty. "That was really sweet," she said feeling guilty.

He shook his head as if to clear it. What was he missing? He had no idea what was going on, but it was clear he'd misread what was between her and Taliaferro. He'd expected a brave face over devastation. Instead, she seemed exasperated.

She sucked on her bottom lip. He found himself getting inappropriately turned on.

"Michael and I were just messing around," she hesitantly confessed as she handed the tablet back to him.

"Okay," he said. "That's good." He ignored the pang of jealousy he felt at thought of her, "messing around" with Taliaferro. "I just thought you should know. I guess I assumed things were more serious than they actually were."

She looked away and started tugging a curl that had come loose from her ponytail, winding it around her finger and releasing it. He found himself transfixed by the motion.

"I don't mean messing around like that," she said, letting the curl go and getting up from her seat. She started pacing restlessly.

Suddenly hopeful, he nodded even though he had no idea what the hell was going on.

"I don't like being told what to do," she stated as if that explained things.

"Okay," he said still not sure where she was going with this.

"Michael really doesn't like to be told what to do, so when you went all lord of the manor and told us to stay away from each other..." she trailed off.

"You decided to jerk my chain?" he asked as the truth dawned on him. There never had been anything between those two but friendship and a shared desire for a little revenge. He felt a bubble of laughter well up in his gut. He would have expected Taliaferro to think that such a prank was hilarious, but it was a side of Emily he hadn't anticipated.

She nodded, "I know it sounds like middle school, and looking back, it was dumb and unprofessional, but at the time, it seemed like a great idea. I don't even know why I let it go on except I didn't really know how to stop it gracefully."

She trembled and plopped down on the couch next to him, and then, she was laughing too. He felt all of the tension leave the room.

She took a few deep breaths to control herself, but when she looked up and her eyes met his, they both started laughing again because it was all so ridiculous. She started to turn away, and he put his hand on her shoulder. As soon as he touched her, a new tension entered the room. Their eyes locked.

Hers were wet with hilarity, but as he and Emily looked at one another, the broad grin fell away from her face, and her expression softened into surprise and anticipation.

He leaned forward, giving her plenty of time to retreat, but she just sat there transfixed as he bent to kiss her. It started gently, a press of lips to lips, but her mouth was soft and yielding, and it didn't stay gentle for long. He kissed her harder, kissed her like he'd wanted to from the day she'd fallen into his life. He hands were in her hair. Her fingers toyed with the short hair at his nape and teased along his neck.

He moaned into her mouth and pushed her back onto the couch under him. Her body was as soft and yielding as he'd dreamed. One of his hands travelled down her side to her waist. She arched against him, and he was pushing up her shirt to touch the skin of her hip.

Suddenly, as if his touching of her bare skin had broken the spell, she was pulling away, pushing him off of her. He let her up, breathing like he had just run a race. She sat up unsteadily and visibly struggled to get her own breathing under control.

Emily's brain fought a quick, nasty battle with her hormones, and unfortunately, managed to edge out a victory. She couldn't do this. No matter how much she wanted to have sex with him she couldn't do it right now, not like this. She panted, trying to get her breath back as he looked at her confused and waited for her to explain.

"Sorry," she said, not liking the tremor in her voice. "That was a little too fast for me."

He groaned and put his head in his hands, getting his own breath back before he looked back up at her. He tried what she suspected was supposed to be a reassuring smile. It came out a little crooked. "No, I'm sorry I made you uncomfortable. I didn't mean to take things that fast. It just was kind of crazy for a minute there."

She shook her head and smiled back, "Oh, you didn't make me uncomfortable the way you mean." She took a deep breath and confessed, "It's just that I've only had sex with my fiancé' and one other person in my life, and it's not something I jump into even when I really want to. Plus, we're business associates." Before he could say anything, she said, "I know people have sex and it means nothing, but I don't think I can do that. I think it would be impossible to work together after, well, for me anyway."

"Oh," was all he could manage as he was at a loss for words.

Well, that combined with the adolescent silliness she and Michael had pulled had probably sunk the small chance she'd had with him.

He sat up straighter and looked at her consideringly. "Okay then, we'll date."

She narrowed her eyes at his arrogance, but she couldn't hide her surprise. Spontaneous sex, she could see him justifying, but an actual relationship was a whole other kind of risk.

"Really?" she asked.

"Well, you did imply you really wanted to go farther, so I just assumed you might want to date first since, apparently, fast sex is off the table for now." He gave an exaggerated sigh. "And that really is a damn shame."

She was overwhelmed, "What about the business relationship?"

"I haven't been really good about keeping things all business from the beginning," he admitted with humor lacing his voice. "So, I'm pretty sure this can't make it worse. We can keep things separate and private."

"You want to date and hide it?" she asked feeling deflated. When he'd said he wanted to date even though she didn't want to have sex right away, she'd felt cautious excitement, but it was dissipating quickly.

"No," he was quick to answer, but she thought she heard hesitation in his voice. "That's not what I meant. I just didn't want you to feel uncomfortable with the people at Indulgence. I just wanted us to get used to each other without all of the assumptions and speculations."

"You're right, it would be good to take that part slow," she admitted. Part of her was nervous at the idea of secrecy, but she was a private person, and the thought of dealing with the kind of scrutiny at work that came with dating the boss made her feel physically ill.

"Plus," he teased with his eyes sparkling with mischief, "anticipation can be fun too."

He stood up, "I should go, but let's have dinner this week, and then... who knows."

She nodded and walked him to the door.

He turned and leaned down, his face close to hers. She thought he would kiss her again. She wanted him to kiss her again, and by his grin, he knew she wanted it. Instead he turned his head to the side. She felt his breath warm against her ear and she shivered. He whispered, "I'm already anticipating." Then, before she could say anything, he was gone.

Her legs felt like jelly as she locked the door and leaned back against it hard. Then, she groaned.

She knew she'd made the right call about not jumping right into sex especially with someone she had a business relationship with, but hell, Nick Hawkins was hot when he was not trying to be bossy. When he was being considerate and seductive, he was almost irresistible. Actually, she probably deserved a medal for turning him down. Sadly, what she was going to get was a cool shower and a lonely bed.

Chapter 15

Nick was humming to himself when he got to the office Monday morning. He was done banging his head against the wall. Ever since he'd met Emily, he'd been acting like an idiot, and now, he was enjoying the feeling of giving in to temptation. He grinned when he thought about her expression when he hadn't kissed her on the way out. If he'd had any problems with his ego, that look would have gone a long way towards solving them.

He was even happy that they hadn't had sex. Well, he hadn't been at all happy at the time, but now, he thought it had been for the best. At first, her relative lack of experience freaked him out a little, but while normally, that kind of confession would have had him running for the hills, he was oddly okay with it coming from her. It was a new kind of challenge, and he loved a good challenge.

He walked past his assistant's empty desk. It was rare that he beat Molly into the office. He got a lot of work done at night, so he usually came in late and stayed late. He had plans tonight, though, so he wanted to be sure to get everything done. The last thing he wanted to intrude on his date with Emily was work. In fact, they'd made a pact about. Dates were going to be work-free zones.

As he pushed the door to his office open, he heard a shocked gasp and was startled to see Michelle by his desk. It wasn't unusual for her to come in early, but what was she doing in his office at this hour?

"Did we have a meeting I've forgotten?" he asked her.

She straightened from the papers she'd been looking at and shook her head. "No, sorry," she said clearly a little flustered. "I just didn't expect you to be in until later, and I wanted to get started on some of the projections for the launches. Molly never emailed me the final figures, and I thought the working copy was in here," she explained.

He shrugged, "Did you find it?"

She shook her head, "I guess it will have to wait until she gets in. While I've got you, I was wondering if you were still set on ignoring this latest scandal of Taliaferro's."

He sighed. Michelle wanted to issue some kind of statement, but their PR people thought it would be best to just let it go since it didn't actually impact any of their lines. "I am. I know you disagree, but I think the right call is just to stay above it and hope we benefit from the increased attention. It will turn some people off, but the scandal doesn't involve food, and Lachlan is pretty sure we'll gain a lot more business than we'll lose. He says we'll only hurt ourselves by commenting."

Michelle nodded but didn't look convinced. She started to leave. He heard her muttering about the updated figures she needed.

"Michelle," he called as he remembered something else he needed from her.

She turned back to him. "Yes?"

"While I've got you, I wondered if you had an update for me on our leak. Do we have any idea how the Taliaferro deal got out so fast?" After that information had leaked, he'd been furious and had tasked Michelle with getting to the bottom of it. They were already struggling to undo the damage caused by some bad press, and they did not need internal leaks. He had faith that if the person who had leaked the information could be found, Michelle would find him or her.

She shook her head. "Sorry. I haven't been able to trace it. If you want me to be less discreet, maybe, I could find something, but as long as we want to keep it quiet, it's going to be slow going I'm afraid."

"Damn," he cursed. "No, I don't want to turn this into a witch hunt. Just keep me updated."

She nodded and left his office.

He sat at his desk and fired up his laptop. After making a note to Molly to keep trying Taliaferro and to get Michelle the figures she needed, he settled in to deal with his email. When he saw the disaster that was his inbox, he groaned but forced himself to deal with the task at hand. He needed to get this under control if he wanted to get away at a reasonable hour tonight. Unfortunately, his mind was already on the dinner he had planned with Emily, so it was going to be a very long day.

"So, how was breakfast with the absent-minded professor?" Robin asked. They were sitting in Robin's living room eating takeout pizza and working on plans for their prepared food recipes in anticipation of a meeting with Joe. Robin claimed that her baby was a pizza fan, and since she'd gone from a flat stomach to impressive baby bump in what Emily assumed was a record amount of time, Emily had no reason to doubt her.

"Fine, he was 15 minutes late and didn't see what the big deal was. Typical Pete."

"Good thing you didn't end up marrying him then." Robin wiped her mouth then grabbed another slice.

"Definitely," Emily said with conviction. "He's dating someone new, a grad student in his department. I think it's serious."

Really, Pete had seemed genuinely happy. He'd been puzzled when Emily's, "boyfriend" hadn't shown up and really confused when she'd tried to explain that Michael wasn't her boyfriend, just a friend with a strange sense of humor. Truthfully, when she'd attempted to tell the story, it hadn't even made sense to her, and she'd lived it. Fortunately, the topic hadn't held Pete's interest for long. As soon as she'd given him an opening, he'd started talking away about his latest research project and his new girlfriend, who was working on it with him. Emily shuddered to think of their life together. If his new girlfriend was as absent minded as Pete, their house would probably fall apart around them. Thankfully, that was no longer her concern.

Robin shot her a questioning look, probably expecting her to fall apart. "Are you okay with that?"

Emily shrugged. "Remember, I dumped him."

"But still, you guys were engaged. It's okay to be sad about it."

"We've been broken up for five years. He has a right to move on." Emily took a bite of her pizza and made a face. She hated green peppers on pizza. She must have grabbed part of Robin's half by accident. She put it down.

Robin glared at her. She was pretty possessive of her slices these days, but she let it slide in favor the topic at hand. "But still, you guys were engaged for a long time."

Emily attempted to eat around the peppers. She'd try to pick them off if she didn't think Robin would beat her with the greasy box for doing it. "Do you want me to get upset?"

"No," Robin said. Her eyes narrowed. "What's going on with you? Two months ago when Pete called to check up on you, you were a wreck."

Breaking up had been the right decision, without a doubt, but there had always been guilt and regret mixed up with the relief and anger. Many times wanting to get back together with him but only to have the companionship which was never the answer and Emily knew that in her heart. Finally, Nick had given Emily what she needed all this time, the ability to let go.

Emily paused. Here was her opening. She knew she had to tell Robin about Nick, but she dreaded her friend's reaction. She took a deep breath. "I made out with Nick Hawkins," she blurted out before she lost her nerve.

"Emily," Robin said stunned. She stared open mouthed for a few uncomfortable seconds.

"Say something please."

Robin shook her head and tried to speak. When nothing came out at first, she held up her hand, took a deep breath and said, "I don't know what to say.

I'm not sure whether to congratulate you or shake you. Right now, I'm leaning toward both."

Emily sighed, "Neither would do much good."

"God Em. This could be a mess you know?"

Emily nodded glumly. "I know. He seems to think we can keep the business and the dating separate and it sounded doable while in the moment."

Robin's eyes widened. "Dating? So, it wasn't just a random make-out session?"

"It was, but then, it was more." Emily shrugged. "Who the hell knows. It just felt really great." She paused and then smiled uncertainly. "It felt right."

Robin sighed. "But you didn't actually sleep with him?"

Emily shook her head. "We're in business together. I thought he'd play it off and bolt, but he said he wants us to date."

Robin looked torn between disapproval and excitement, "Do you think that's a good idea?"

"No," Emily said honestly. "I think it's probably not, but Robin, as soon as he saw those pictures of Michael and Selena on the Web, he rushed to find me before he even tried to sort out the business side of things. He didn't want me to hear about it on TV or read it on the Internet. He was so sweet. There was no 'told you so' or complaints about bad publicity for the business. He just was worried I'd be devastated, and he wanted to console me."

Robin made the kind of whimpering sound usually reserved for Liftetime movie marathons.

"Are you tearing up?" Emily asked.

Robin swatted her, "It's hormones. At this point, I cry at telephone commercials." She sniffed and then continued, "But now, I get why you couldn't say no. I actually can't believe you didn't fall into bed with him then and there." She paused and grinned. I would have."

Emily laughed. "It wasn't easy." She took a bite of her pizza, peppers and all. "He whispered something in my ear about anticipation before he left." She shivered at the memory.

Robin groaned theatrically. "You're either crazy or trying for sainthood."

"No kidding," Emily agreed. Then, she looked at Robin with a serious expression. "I've been thinking about it, and I believe we can actually keep this separate and have it not impact the business relationship, but if you're worried, I won't let it go any farther."

"Are you crazy Em? No, I'm not going to lie. It's scary, but we have a signed contract, and you're both grown-ups. Plus, Nick Hawkins is freaking hot, and I'm hormonal." She paused to chew her pizza. "Since, I'm married; I'll just have to live vicariously through you. I do expect details, though, lots and lots of details."

Emily gave her a quick hug. Her eyes burned with unshed tears. "We'll see.

Robin threatened, "If you don't deliver, I'll sick Mia on you."

Emily groaned.

Chapter 16

"I thought you liked things spicy," Emily teased as Nick walked her to the car.

"I do," he countered. "I just like to taste my food a little instead of using it to singe my tongue."

This was their fifth date in the past three weeks, and to his credit, he'd been a perfect gentleman. Emily was starting to wish he would be less of one. Tonight, she'd taken him to one of her favorite Thai places where the options were hot, hotter and nuclear. That had been her idea of a hint, but it had probably been too subtle. She'd also worn a short blue sun dress that clung to her in a way Robin had assured her was hot without being completely slutty. That was a less subtle hint. He'd definitely eyed her appreciatively and given her a million small touches that were halfway to making her insane, he still wasn't giving in.

"You could have warned me," he complained as he hit the keyless entry.

"I did. You just didn't listen," she reminded him as she got in the car through the passenger door he held open for her.

"I'm pretty sure you didn't," he said as he leaned over and fastened her seatbelt for her.

"What am I helpless?" she asked, but her voice came out breathy and flirty instead of annoyed. It was all she could do to suppress a shiver of pleasure as his hands brushed over her.

He gave her a teasing grin. "Just trying to be a gentleman."

She groaned and just wanted to attack him. She wondered if that was his plan. Maybe, since she'd turned him down, he needed her to actually tell him it was time. She wasn't sure she was ready to do that tonight, but she was getting close.

"So, what do think about a movie this weekend?" he asked as he got in the car and shut his door. He ran a hand over her knee lightly before taking the wheel.

"As long as there aren't any killer robots," she said, her voice sounding a little squeaky. Last weekend, he'd insisted she was going to love the Transformers franchise. After one and a half movies, she'd insisted he was deranged.

"You started to come around in the end," he said all too innocently.

She shot him a glare. Midway through movie number two, they'd started making out, and while it had been great fun, just when she was getting worked up, he cheerfully suggested more popcorn. She was pretty sure he'd planned it to torture her. She'd considered knocking him upside the head with the remote control but had somehow restrained herself.

"You're deluded," she told him. "We're seeing something good, maybe a Jane Austen marathon."

He made a long-suffering sound. "One Jane Austen movie I can do, but not a marathon."

She relented. "Lord of the Rings, then."

"Oh yeah," he agreed. "I even have those."

"I have the director's cuts on DVD," she said with a grin.

"You are possibly the perfect woman."

"Plus, Viggo Mortensen is so hot as Aragorn," she sighed.

"Well except for your mean streak," he teased. "But we'll work on that." He pulled the car away from the curb.

"You're not a nice person," Michael told her. He'd cornered her in one of the conference rooms at Indulgence where they'd just finished a meeting. The Sweet Life line, which was officially called Guiltless Indulgence, was really coming together. In addition to pre-made treats, they were offering a few recipe kits and all of the people working on them seemed pretty excited.

"Because I called you a moron?" she asked, but he looked so sad that she relented. "Okay, fine, you can hang out at my place to dodge the attention, but you have to promise to stop teasing Nick."

A wicked look replaced the kicked-puppy expression he'd been wearing.

"I mean it," she said.

He held up his hand and gave her a mock pout. Then his face turned serious, and he said, "Fine, but you should be careful with Hawkins. He's a player."

She rolled her eyes at him. "Says the man who tried to pick me up in a lobby the first time he laid eyes on me and is now tabloid fodder for hooking up with an engaged semi celebrity in a nightclub."

"That's different," he protested, but he looked uncomfortable with the subject. "And the Selena thing was a mistake. We always flirt, but we were drunk and it went too far. It'll blow over."

"I guess." Considering the attention span of most tabloid reporters, Emily thought he was probably right. Michael was a minor celebrity among foodies and reality show viewers, and Selena was slightly more well known, but neither one of them was an A-list star.

Before he could say anymore, there was the sound of someone clearing his throat behind her. Emily turned to see Joe wearing an annoyed look on his face.

"Mr. Hawkins will be waiting in his office," Joe said. Lately, he always looked disapproving. Emily would be willing to bet he thought she was sleeping with Michael despite the Selena incident. She resisted the urge to laugh and wondered what his reaction would be if he knew she was actually dating his boss.

"We'll be right there," Michael said. They were supposed to meet to go over a cooking spot on a local morning talk show. Nick was doing an interview, and she, Robin and Michael were doing a cooking demonstration. Well, Michael and Robin were doing the cooking, and she was talking about adapting recipes for specific dietary needs. For some reason, the whole idea seemed to annoy the normally calm Joe.

Joe just stood there as if he was prepared to wait all day. Emily sighed and picked up her bag before heading past him to the door. Michael followed her, and Joe closed the door behind them. Apparently, he was taking on the role of babysitter today. There definitely was some hostility toward Michael since the Selena incident. Apparently, Selena was the office favorite, and they were blaming Michael for causing her problems. While Emily definitely believed Michael deserved his share of the blame, the fact was that he wasn't the one with a fiancé.

"Where's the third musketeer?" Nick asked as he caught up with them on the way to his office.

"You're late, Mr. Hawkins," Emily observed with a pointed look at Joe. He ignored her in favor of glaring at Michael, and she continued, "Robin's probably already waiting for us."

Nick shrugged. He started to reach for her and checked the gesture. She suppressed a smile, and then, she had to swallow a gasp as he grabbed her arm. She looked around, but except for Joe and Michael, no one was in the hall. It was the end of the day, and most of the staff had gone home.

"We'll be right there," he told the two men.

Michael looked like he wanted to laugh, but he just walked past them into Nick's office, and Joe followed.

"Way to be subtle," Emily joked, but she was also trying not to laugh.

After a quick look around, Nick guided her back to the wall for a quick but thorough kiss. Just when she was starting to not care where they were, he broke it off and reached up to brush a finger over her lips, which she was sure were swollen. His expression held a possessive satisfaction.

"And what was that for?" she asked, noting that her voice had gone suddenly husky.

"Just because I had to," he said with a smile. He looked more relaxed and tousled than usual. Since it was the end of the workday, and theirs was the last meeting, he'd even ditched his usual tie.

With a smile of her own, she brushed her fingers over the exposed skin revealed by the open top button of his shirt. He sucked in a breath, but her fingers stilled when she saw the edge of a design. Intriguing.

"A tattoo?" She asked. At his nod, she said, "You are full of surprises."

"I love to keep you on your toes," he said, taking her hand and starting to pull her toward his office and their meeting.

She resisted, and he stopped shooting her a questioning look. "Don't tease," she said. "What's the tattoo?"

"We'll be late," he said and laughed at the glare she shot him.

"Nick. Come on. Tell me."

He shook his head slowly. "Let's call it an incentive," he said in a low voice, bending his head close to her ear.

"An incentive?" she asked, blushing at how her voice had just quavered.

He nodded solemnly. "Yeah, if I don't tell you, it gives you more incentive to want to get my shirt off, and I can promise you're going to have to work for it."

"Oh yeah?" she asked and then smiled slowly. "And what if I promised to reciprocate?"

He gave her a long lazy look that made her feel warm right down to her core. "That might work."

"So?" she asked.

"What here?" he said feigning shock. "Okay, but it could get weird. You first."

She huffed in mock annoyance, "That's not what I meant. You tell me and I'll make it worth your while ...later."

"Tempting," he said, "but I don't take IOUs. I'm way too good a businessman. I get paid up front and I'm very, very expensive."

He laughed at the choked, squeaky sound she made and tugged her toward his office.

"Nothing yet?" Mia asked disbelievingly.

Emily shook her head and took a drink of her wine. Robin had made good on her threat and sicced Mia on her. Well, Robin had invited them over for wine and an assortment of snacks, but since both Mia and Robin had commenced with the sex interrogation as soon as she'd walked in the door, Emily wasn't willing to cut her much slack.

"You're going to have to tell him you're ready," Robin said between bites of a terrifying looking sandwich that seemed to mainly consist of chicken, cheese and half a bottle of dressing. Emily knew better than to comment on it. The last time Mia had said anything about one of Robin's food choices, she'd almost lost a few body parts.

"Definitely, forget about the subtle hints," Mia said. "Men are almost never subtle when it comes to sex, but you might not want to just blurt out that you want to screw like you're telling him what you want to order for dinner," she said. Then, seeing that Robin was about to argue, she continued quickly before her friend could swallow the food in her mouth, "I'm not saying don't come right out and tell him what you want. I'm just saying you should set the mood first. He obviously likes games, so if you're going to play, you should win."

Emily wasn't sure she wanted to play at all. Oh, she wanted to sleep with Nick. God, she wanted to sleep with Nick. Lately, it was the number one topic on her mind, but she was very much afraid that there had been too much build up for it. She worried that with her minimal experience, she'd never be able to meet his high expectations in the bedroom and that he'd never be able to meet hers outside of it.

When she wasn't obsessing about sex, she was thinking about the fact that Nick hadn't told her he was negotiating with Michael even though he knew she'd have a problem with it. Then, she'd remember that his company had only wanted her and Robin to develop a line because Indulgence had an honesty problem. She'd even taken to second guessing his motives for keeping their relationship a secret. She knew that she had issues with trust, but somehow, no matter what she told herself, she couldn't completely relax and enjoy the situation. In the end, what scared her the most was that she'd grown attached to Nick. She wanted to sleep with him, but that wasn't all. She just wanted him, and she was worried that he was going to break her heart.

She stared into her drink, her thoughts spinning a million miles a minute.

"Hey now," Mia said. "I didn't mean you should mope. Just tell him you want to screw if you want. I just thought it might be fun and hot to make him show that he's as worked up as you are before you seal the deal." She shrugged. "Lady's choice of course."

Emily forced a weak smile. Really, that did sound hot. In theory, she was sexually liberated, and she could tell Nick she was ready to take their relationship to the next level, but Mia was right that the issue had become a battle of wills. And, she admitted to herself that she'd been mostly letting him win. When he touched her, her brain just shut down. She gave Mia a considering look. "Okay, genius, why don't you tell me how I win then?"

She swallowed hard, a little afraid of the grin Mia shot her.

Chapter 17

Mia, Emily reflected, might be good at seducing men herself, but her techniques were probably not ideal for the general public. While Emily liked to think she was a sexually liberated woman, the fact was that most of that sexual liberation had never been tested in the real world. Emily had decided to modify Mia's outrageous suggestions for the more inhibited crowd.

She squirmed uncomfortably. The lace panties and bra her friend had talked her into buying were itchy against her skin. At least, she'd flat out refused the thong. She wore thongs under pants to avoid showing panty lines, but wearing a thong under a skirt just felt weird to her. She'd almost rather wear nothing. Mia had thought that that idea had merit, but Emily had decided to save that for later. Instead, she went with bikini panties in violet lace with a matching demi bra under her simple blue tank dress. Her hair was down around her shoulders and she felt sexy.

Finding Love in the Sweet Life

When she opened the door and Nick walked in, she almost forgot to breathe. She'd always found him handsome, but since they'd started dating, she sometimes looked at him and couldn't believe he was real and really into her. Tonight, she'd offered to cook him dinner at her place because she figured she'd be more comfortable at home. She'd also taken shameful advantage of the fact that her two best friends were chefs to get out of doing most of the actual cooking.

"You look amazing," he said, his eyes warm and appreciative as they took in her body in the dress. He gave her a soft kiss hello and then, brushed past her to the kitchen. She did her best to get her breathing under control. She was not going to melt at his feet before they'd even had salad.

"Do you want wine?" he asked. "I brought a Spanish red that's supposed to go well with mushrooms."

"And how did you know we were having mushroom and herb pasta?" she asked.

"Well, I know you don't eat a lot of meat, so mushrooms seemed logical."

"Wow," she said trying to look impressed before adding, "you are so full of bullshit I don't know why you don't reek. Who's the traitor?"

He grinned unrepentantly, "I might have called Robin." At her mock glare, he added with laughter in his voice, "You know, just to check up on her."

He handed her a glass of wine and poured one for himself. She took an experimental sip. "Oh this is good. Sometimes red wine has a little too much acid for me, but this is nice."

"It's possible that I had a little help with the selection," he confessed.

"Uh huh," she said, starting to relax. With the thought that tonight was finally *the* night she'd been tense and jumpy from most of the day, but a little wine and some light flirting had her feeling relaxed. "Remind me never to tell Robin anything again."

He laughed softly, "Maybe to get even you'll have to do something worth not telling her about."

"Maybe so," Emily said before giving him what she hoped was an enigmatic smile. She took a sip of her wine and laughed. "You're a very brave man you know."

"Am I?"

It was her turn to laugh. She jiggled her wine glass a little. "I have a very bad history with you and red wine."

"I'm going to go out on a limb and say you've more than made up for it."

"How presumptuous," she said trying and failing to sound disapproving.

"I'm not presuming anything," he said innocently. "I just meant this dinner more than makes up for the fact that you ruined my favorite shirt."

"Liar," she said, but she was grinning like a fool.

His smile widened, and almost before she could react, he had set his wine glass on the table and deftly extracted hers from her hand and set it down as well. Then, he put his arms around her and starting kissing her soft lips.

At her eager acceptance, he moaned into her mouth and pulled her tighter. His hand moved from her waist to her bottom, and it was her turn to moan into his mouth. In record time, her back was against the kitchen island, and he was kissing her like a starving man at his first meal in days. She was kissing him back with no reservations. All of her worries had faded to a barely audible hum, and there was only his mouth on hers, his body pressing into hers.

She moved restlessly against him, arching her hips up and felt him gasp against her lips. His mouth left hers, moving down her neck. Her breath came hard as she felt the cool air on her swollen lips and his hot kiss against her neck. He shifted, his body pushing harder into hers, and she winced, crying out in sudden pain as the edge of the counter dug into her back.

At her protest, he released her and backed away breathing unsteadily. She straightened and looked up at him. His eyes, she was relieved to see, were as glassy and lost as she imagined hers were. She didn't want to be the only one so affected by a kiss.

"Sorry," he said, his breath uneven and his voice impossibly deep. "I got carried away. Are you okay?"

She nodded. "I'm fine," she said, her own voice husky in her ears. "I think maybe the kitchen counter thing just works better in movies." She rubbed her back.

He gave her a considering look, "I bet it could work with practice."

"Let's save the advanced stuff for later. Tonight, I want a bed."

He swallowed hard, "Now?"

"Did you want me to serve dinner?" she asked, her voice not even close to even.

He shook his head and started toward her again. Screw dinner. She gave him a welcoming smile. They could eat it later. Maybe, they'd eat between rounds.

Before he could carry her off to her bed to do what they'd been dancing around since she'd first spilled wine on him, the buzz of the intercom shattered the perfect mood. She thought about ignoring it, but whoever was at the door was keeping up a steady pressure, a sign that he or she was determined.

"Sorry," Emily said ducking out of his grip. "I'll get rid of whoever it is." If Michael was downstairs, she was going to murder him slowly.

She hit the button, and in a shaky voice said, "Yes."

"Let me up." Michael's voice was unmistakable.

"I'm going to rip his head off," Nick said through gritted teeth.

"Not if I get to him first." She pushed the button and said to Michael, "Go away."

"Em, I... please let me up." He sounded so far from his cocky self that she was torn.

She looked at Nick helplessly. He groaned, made an, "as you wish" gesture and sank onto the couch his head in his hands.

She buzzed Michael up. By the time he reached her door, she had done her best to straighten her dress and compose herself. Nick's hair still looked pretty finger mussed, and he seemed to have no interest in putting on any facade for her very much unwelcome guest.

"What?" she asked none too charitably as she opened the door and then sucked in a breath when she got a good look at him. "Michael, what happened to you?" There was dried blood around his nose, and his left eye seemed on the way to swelling shut. His white tee was ripped and seemed to have dirt and maybe blood on it.

"Jealous fiancé,'" he said obviously trying to sound light and failing miserably. "Not my first, but baby doll, remind me next time to stay away from women who are engaged to guys who moonlight as Mack trucks."

"Stop trying to be funny and sit down before you fall down," she said steering him into the kitchen and depositing him in one of the chairs.

Nick was already rifling through her freezer. "Perfect," he said pulling out a bag of peas. "These are the best because they'll mold to your face."

As soon as she was sure he was settled, she went to sink and dampened a paper towel. Over his protests, she used it to clean his face.

"I think you should go to the ER. You might have a concussion," she told him.

"Nah," he said, wincing a little. "I've had worse. This is just a few banged up ribs, an epic black eye, bloody nose and bruised jaw. I'll be fine. I just didn't want to go back to my hotel. After the mess with me and Selena, if anyone saw me like this, they'd have their phones out for a picture to sell to a tabloid before I could blink."

"Did anyone see you?" Nick was pacing in her kitchen, frantically texting on his phone. Apparently, he was looking at this as a potential PR problem and was trying for damage control. She felt a pang of annoyance at that. There was a hurt man in front of him, and he immediately thought about the PR implications of the situation. She quashed the thought. He'd gotten him ice before he'd started texting, and she supposed that's what it took to run a business like Indulgence successfully.

Michael shook his head and then winced. He blinked, and took in Emily in her dress, the table set for two, the half-full wine glasses and Nick's somewhat rumpled appearance. He bit out a curse and said, "It looks like I'm interrupting. Sorry. Thanks for getting me cleaned up, I'll just go..."

He started to get up and then winced in pain as Emily eased him back into the chair. "You're not going anywhere like this. You can crash here tonight." She gave Nick an apologetic look, and he shrugged resignedly.

She lowered herself into the chair across from Michael, and Nick sat next to her. "So, I think we can all agree I deserve a good explanation," she told him, her tone making it clear that she was not in the mood for any of his tall tales or sweet talk tonight.

Fortunately, Michael was too exhausted to push her. He told them how Selena's fiancé had found him in a bar where he'd gone to have a beer and insisted on a discussion in the back room. The bar had mysteriously cleared out for the Eagles' newest star, and Michael had been on the receiving end of a beat down and a warning. He claimed he'd held his own or as much of his own as a regular-sized guy with a history of street fights could hold against a professional athlete built like The Hulk. When he'd left the bar, he'd decided a low profile was the best and avoided the crowded hotel lobby in favor of a deserted garage and his rental car.

Emily was annoyed at him for driving in his condition, but Nick seemed pleased that he'd stayed out of the public eye. People might ignore and even appreciate a bit of scandal, but too many incidents like this created a distraction. Nick was annoyed that they were going to have to reschedule or rethink their television spot. Clearly, Michael could not go on the air looking like an accident victim, and by the time they start taping, he was going to have a spectacular shiner.

Once they had finished with explanations, repurposed dinner for two to serve three and gotten Michael as cleaned up as he was going to get, she'd excused herself to change. Nick had watched her disappear into the bedroom, his eyes full of regret.

Once alone, she stripped out of her blue dress and sighed as she caught sight of herself in her sexy undies in the mirror. Sadly, she was the only one who was going to appreciate them tonight. She replaced the bra with a tank top that had a built-in bra. She couldn't sleep in a regular bra, but she was too big up top to parade around two men in just a t-shirt without looking like she was angling for something kinky. Over her tank, she put on a light gray tee, and she slid a pair of plaid sleep shorts over her panties. She'd gone from looking for trouble to dormitory chic in a matter of minutes.

When she returned to the living room with bedding a pillow for the couch, both men were still at the table. Nick gave her a quick once over, his gaze lingering on her bare legs. Michael must be worn out because he didn't even tease. He just gave her an apologetic smile.

"You're hurt, so you can take my bed," she told Michael. "I'll sleep in the office. There's a couch in there. My traumatized cat is hiding under it."

Both men looked at her as if she had gone insane. Michael shook his head, "No sense me putting you both out when the couch is better than I deserve."

She started to protest, but Nick said, "Knock if you need anything," grabbed her arm and pulled her toward the bedroom.

She barely had time to squeak out, "Good night," before he'd shut the door and pushed her up against it. He gave her fast hard kiss that was over before she'd had a chance to decide how to respond to it.

She glared at him and hissed, "I am not sleeping with you with Michael in the next room," she hissed.

"Well, I thought we'd get some sleep, but if you have other ideas, I'm game." He eyed her considering the options, "Hopefully you can keep quiet. No, I take that back. Scream all you want. He deserves it."

"You know that's not what I meant. It's just that it might be kind of hard," she winced at the unintended double entendre but continued before he could comment, "for us to sleep in the same bed tonight."

"It's going to be hell," he agreed. "But if you think I'm leaving you here alone with him, you're out of your mind."

"You know we're just friends."

"Still not happening," he told her. He started to undo his pants.

She squeaked and asked in an urgent whisper, "What are you doing?"

He shot her an annoyed look, "Do you think I'm going to sleep fully dressed? I'm going to strip down to my shorts and t-shirt. Don't worry, I can defend myself if you attack me in a fit of hormone-induced mania at the sight."

"That," she assured him annoyed, "won't be a problem."

She had possibly spoken too soon. When his pants and dress shirt were folded on top of her dresser and he stood in a pair of boxer briefs and a v-neck tee that clung to the hard planes of his chest and abdomen, she felt suddenly warm. She bit her lip hard to keep from sighing. He closed his eyes as if in pain, and she blushed as she realized that her interest had made him start to get aroused in return.

She got up and dodged his hand as she walked past him.

"Where are you going?" he asked.

"Thermostat," she told him. "I forgot to set it."

"Colder is definitely a good idea," he said with feeling.

It was going to be a very long night.

Chapter 18

Nick moaned and pulled his pillow over his face to shut out the light shining in through the window. Window? His bedroom window didn't get morning sun. "Emily's bed," he thought groggily. "I'm in Emily's bed." He moved his hand to reach for her to confirm that he really was in bed with her, but he could only feel empty covers. He eased the pillow off of his face, wincing at the bright light.

He sat up groaning a little and registered the sound of running water coming from the bathroom. He rubbed his eyes and stretched the aches of sleeping in an unfamiliar bed from his knotted muscles. It really was a bad idea to fall asleep when you were that keyed up. He'd lain in bed listening to Emily breathe less than a foot away, and it had taken every bit of willpower he had not to reach for her and convince her that quick, quiet sex with another man a paper-thin wall away was a fabulous idea. Only the fact that they had waited too long to have a first time like that had stopped him from trying it.

"Good morning," Emily said a little shyly standing in the bedroom doorway. In her plaid shorts and tee with her hair in a messy ponytail, she looked like a college coed. He felt kind of dirty for being so turned on by it.

"Morning," he said getting up from the bed. He gave her a quick kiss on the cheek with a closed mouth so as not to subject her to his morning breath. Her face was damp as if she'd just washed it, and she smelled like toothpaste.

"Taliaferro still out?" A few times during the night she'd gotten up to check on Michael because she'd been worried he could have a concussion. After the first time, Nick had pretended to sleep through it. She'd been so careful about getting up quietly that he hadn't wanted to make her feel bad about waking him up, but really, he had been aware of pretty much every movement and every breath she'd taken for most of the night.

She tensed and swallowed. "He left already. I offered to drive him, but he just wanted to go. He said he was fine. I mean he looked like he lost a fight with a truck, but he seemed okay, and he was completely coherent. He's going to check into a new hotel and send for his stuff just in case anyone's staking out his old place." She looked worried. "He's not a major celebrity, so it's probably overkill, but he seemed really touchy about pictures of him looking beat up potentially ending up online."

"Sounds like he's got things covered," Nick tried to reassure her. "I'm sure you're right, and he's got things under control." He was pretty sure that that wasn't actually true, but there was nothing she could do about it now. He also felt like he should probably be more concerned about Taliaferro, but he could not stop thinking about how perfect the evening had almost become before the unwelcomed interruption.

She nodded, not looking entirely convinced and then said, "I'll try him later to make sure everything is okay.

He gave her what he hoped was a reassuring smile, but his brain was still stuck on the half-dressed woman in front of him and all of the options that an empty apartment afforded them. Feeling those possibilities settle over him, he bit back a moan of anticipation.

Emily heard the bathroom door and took a shaky breath. Her stomach churned with a mix of nerves and anticipation. They had been building to this for a long time. If Michael hadn't burst in last night, they would probably be curled around each other right now sleeping contentedly instead of keyed up nearly to the point of insanity.

"Hi," Nick said as he walked back in the room still in his shirt and shorts. He ran his hand over his jaw and gave her a rueful look, "I couldn't shave. If it's a problem..."

He trailed off as she shook her head and stood. "Not a problem," she assured him barely recognizing her own voice. She crossed to him, her eyes never straying from his, and raised her hand running it over his rough jaw. "Never a problem," her voice sounded husky, sexy and foreign in her own ears.

She felt him shudder and saw the expression in his eyes shift from hope to something hotter and darker, from uncertain anticipation to the look of a man secure in the knowledge that the woman he wanted was his for the taking. She barely had time to process that look before his mouth was hot on hers. The kiss was thorough, consuming.

She felt his hands skim down her back as she gave into it, moaning into his mouth as his clever hands moved lower to cup her bottom. When she whimpered, he pushed her harder against him, leaving no doubt that he was interested and ready. She squirmed against him making him moan into her mouth and urge her back. The backs of her legs pressed against the bed, and she looked up into his impossibly dark blue eyes and saw only desire.

He reached for the hem of her shirt. Instinctively, she started to help him tug it up before her brain sent out a warning. She pushed against his chest to call a temporary halt. His breathing was hard and his eyes unfocused a he looked down at her.

"What's wrong?" His voice seemed rusty as if with disuse.

She worked to catch her breath and then smiled. "Nothing. Just give me a sec."

He nodded, a look of confusion on his face.

She slipped out of his arms and darted for the bathroom where she'd stashed her newly purchased box of condoms. She was sure he probably had some with him, but she'd wanted to be sure they were covered. They'd been moving fast enough a minute ago that it had occurred to her that both of them were in danger of getting completely carried away, and that was not something she was willing to risk.

When she tossed a few packets on the nightstand, he smiled slowly at her. She sucked her bottom lip and shifted. Didn't want to forget."

"Good call." He pulled his shirt over his head, and she looked him over appreciatively. This was a man who did not skip his gym time. The ink just under his left collarbone caught her gaze, a stylized hourglass with wings. She reached up wanting to trace it with her finger, but before she could touch him, he grabbed her hand and raised it to his mouth, planting an open-mouthed kiss in the center of her palm. He licked the skin lightly. She shivered.

"No fair," she said. "I don't get to touch?"

He shook his head, "Not if you want to this to last," he said, his voice impossibly deep. "Later, you can touch anything you want. Actually, I'll insist on it."

"Deal." She felt her lips curve in a smile as he reached for her again, giving her a swift kiss before reaching for the hem of her shirt and tugging it over her head.

Finding Love in the Sweet Life

For a moment, she felt self-conscious and exposed, but the expression of wonder on his face as he looked down at her bare breasts banished that feeling quickly. Deciding she could bend his no touching rule, she took his hand and guided it to her breast. They both moaned as his hand stroked her.

After that, her brain lost track of details. It was all a blur of hot breath and fevered touches. They tumbled to the bed, both past caring about rushing. His hands shook as he opened the condom wrapper, the simple action seeming to take years. And in the end, it lasted just long enough to drive both of them over the edge together.

A while later, after waking from a nap, Emily lay in Nick's arms feeling satisfied and strangely vulnerable. Waiting to sleep together had felt right and she was sure now she'd made a good call on dating first, but the result was that it had meant a lot more than it would have if she'd just given into the desire between them weeks ago. She sighed telling herself to let it go and enjoy the moment.

He stroked her hair, and she turned and smiled up at him. Wow, he took her breath away. Now, he looked messy and relaxed with sleepy satisfied eyes and a slightly goofy smile. She'd done that. Her smile grew as she felt the wonder of that fact settle over her.

"You ok?"

"Good, just thinking," she said. Her voice sounded a little dreamy, almost drunk.

"Then I must not have done my job." He ran a lock of her dark red hair through his fingers.

She sighed. "If you'd done any better, I wouldn't be able to move." She watched his fingers play over the lock of her hair and shivered.

He laughed knowingly. "That's the goal next time them."

"Overachiever," she breathed and laughed a little in return. She turned over to face him fully, half sprawled on top of his big, warm body. She ran her fingers lightly over the tattoo that sat just below his left collarbone. "It's beautiful," she told him tracing the lines of the design and delighting in his small shiver of response.

"Thanks." He started to pull her down for a kiss.

She resisted. At his questioning look, she said, "Not so fast. I want the story."

He sighed. "You want a boring story instead of more sex?"

She gave him a challenging grin. "I want a story and more sex."

"Greedy," he said and took a deep slightly shaky breath. There was an unusual vulnerability in the way he looked at her, and the grin he gave her seemed almost forced. "I was 19 and thought it was deep. Now, it seems kind of a cliché."

"Ah," she said, tracing the mark with her finger and then bending to place a quick open-mouth kiss on the decorated patch of skin. "Whoever did it did a good job," she said against his damp skin. She felt his breathing hitch.

He sucked in a breath and then continued, "My dad had died a few years before, and I wanted a reminder that we always have less time than we think." He shrugged and forced a laugh. "I told you it was a cliché. It's the kind of thing that sounds profound as a teenager and embarrasses you as an adult."

She stilled, not sure exactly what to say. Nick had told her his dad had died in a car accident when Nick was a teenager, but he almost never talked about his childhood. She knew that he was close to his mom, who had remarried a few years ago and now lived outside London, but he never talked about their shared past. She'd gotten the sense that the subject was too painful and that his dad's death was one of the reasons he pushed so hard when it came to his business. He wasn't willing to wait for a future he half expected he'd never see. Given his general attitude about waiting, the fact he'd been willing to take their relationship slowly had made her feel like she might be special to him.

Though she was curious, she decided now might not be the best time to dig at painful memories, so she smiled and asked, "Got any more youthful indiscretions? I want to make sure to fully appreciate each one."

His gaze went from sad to heated in a moment. "That's all the ink I have. I could tell you about other places I thought of getting tattooed though if you wanted." He gave her a wicked grin. "It's a really long list, and some of the places are a little embarrassing"

"Oh yeah?"

"I wouldn't want to hold anything back since you're so into full disclosure and all."

"Good, because I intend to be very, very thorough," she said as she moved against him.

"That," he said pulling her more fully on top of him so she could be in no doubt of how on board with the plan he was, "is the best news I've had in weeks."

"You may live to regret it," she told him in mock seriousness.

"Oh, really? And why on earth would I regret it?"

"You said you wanted brunch and at this rate, you may waste away before you get another meal."

"I'll risk it," he told her, pulling her down for a kiss. After that, neither of them thought about food or anything else.

Chapter 19

Emily stroked Sage's soft fur and listened to the cat purr. She knew how the animal felt. After a morning of amazing sex, she and Nick had shared a huge, lazy lunch at a local cafe and now she felt sleepy and content. She really should check her email, deal with her voicemail messages and get some work done, but all she really wanted to do was sit on the couch, pet her cat and enjoy this rare feeling of total relaxation and satisfaction.

She gasped, earning her a dirty look from the cat. Her phone was off. Shit. Sometime after two o'clock, she and Nick had decided to unplug for a few hours and turning off her phone had made her feel deliciously naughty. Unfortunately, she'd gotten distracted and had forgotten to turn it back on. Time to face the music. She lifted it from the end table where she'd tossed it, careful not to dislodge the cat, and switched it on. She did a double take at the number of missed calls and texts she had accumulated in just a few hours, and her stomach sank. What was going on? Before she could check her messages, though, the phone started to ring.

She cursed when she saw who was on the other line. Great. She really did not need her big brother spoiling her mood right now. Sadly, if she ignored him, he'd just call back. If she ignored that, he would call their mother, and as much as she didn't want to talk to Drew right now, she preferred it to a lecture from their mother. She groaned and accepted the call.

"Hi Drew, what's up?"

"Emily, Thank God. I've left you three messages." He sounded slightly frantic.

"I'm sorry. I was busy and didn't notice. Has something happened? Is Laura okay? Mom? " Her raised voice, disturbed the cat on her lap. Sage dug his claws into Emily's leg to show his displeasure and jumped down, presumably to find a stiller, quieter perch.

"Everyone's fine," Drew said sounding almost confused. It was an unaccustomed tone for him. Her brother, the very successful corporate accountant, was more than a bit of a know it all and typically spoke in the form of decrees.

"Then, what happened? My phone's only been off for a couple of hours."

"Ah," he sounded unsure. She was starting to panic. Drew didn't really do unsure. "Well, I heard about the leaked recipes online and some of the outrage. I was putting in a few hours this morning, and one of my colleagues, she's a social media consultant, knew you were my sister, so she asked about it," he said in a rush.

"What? What leaks? Drew, I don't know what you're talking about."

She heard him sigh. "I thought you'd have heard. I was given to understand it's a very big deal in your circles." He cleared his throat.

She rolled her eyes. Drew was in his thirties, but he always managed to sound like a fussy grandfather.

He continued without waiting for her to respond, "Anyway, there's a story on some blog called, The Gluten-Free Life claiming to have the recipes for your new line for Indulgence. The blog owner had some extremely unflattering things to say about them."

"Oh God," she got out. This was bad news. That blog was pretty influential with a large portion of Sweet Life's customer base.

Drew went on, "I would normally not have seen it, but apparently it's being discussed on Twitter, and it was picked up by a food writer for Clearinghouse News. That's where Leslie, our social media consultant, caught it."

Emily felt a little dizzy. The Gluten-Free Life was a popular blog for those with gluten intolerance, but it wasn't well known outside a pretty small circle. Unfortunately, that circle was her customer base, so a negative mention on that blog was bad enough, but if the whole community had decided to discuss some perceived misstep on Twitter, they were in trouble. That Clearinghouse News, one of the most visited sites on the Internet, had picked it up, this could be potentially disastrous.

"Are you sure the problem was with our line?" She still couldn't quite believe it. The recipes she and Robin had developed were solid and based on all of the most up-to-date nutritional standards. Since diet bloggers and commenters lived to disagree, she wouldn't have been surprised if some of them had nits to pick, but she couldn't imagine how any of their work could cause anything like the major scandal her brother claimed was brewing.

"Yes," he sounded reluctant to confirm it. "The story I read mentions your name prominently. That's why Leslie brought it to me in the first place."

"Okay." She was trying not to freak out, but she needed to see these articles right away to assess the situation. "This has to be some kind of misunderstanding. There's literally nothing in the recipes we developed that should be causing this kind of problem."

"I'm sure it is," he said. "I just wanted to make sure you and Robin had adequate representation. Leslie has some ideas about managing this, and she said that you two should think about consulting someone outside of Indulgence to make sure Hawkins doesn't throw you under the bus to save his company's reputation. Apparently, he makes a habit of that."

Part of her wanted to snap at him that Nick would never do that to her, but the part of her that was still bruised and had trouble trusting forced her to ask, "What do you mean a habit?"

As it turned out, even before he had fired Mae Hough for creating a public relations disaster, Nick had garnered a reputation for finding convenient scapegoats whenever there was a PR problem. Drew's source told him that it was likely that most of that reputation was due to sour grapes, but since the rumors were out there, she'd advised Drew to warn his sister to protect herself.

Emily's first instinct was to reassure Drew that Nick wasn't about to throw her, of all people, under the bus, but doing that would require her to talk about their personal relationship. She had a feeling that information would not go over well in the present circumstances. Instead, she took a deep breath, "I'll talk to Robin about it. Right now, I have to figure out what the hell is actually going on."

After assuring him that she would let him know what she found out, she hung up with Drew and checked her phone. In the little time she'd had it off, she had accumulated 35 missed calls, and her inbox had pretty much exploded. It was just her luck that the one day she decided to unplug and enjoy a few quiet hours, everything went to hell.

She swallowed hard and reached for her laptop. Before she could call anyone back and deal with this mess, she needed to know what exactly had caused it. She'd ignored the calls for a few hours, so 15 more minutes wasn't likely to hurt anything.

After reading the original blog article and some of the resultant debate, she concluded that the original author had had every right to be critical. The leaked recipes were gluten free, but they were lazy. They were packed with sugar and fat and lacked any creativity or depth of flavor. Certainly, none of them would produce anything that had any right to be called gourmet food. The problem was that the recipes on the blog, which supposedly came from a source inside Indulgence, were not for any of the products Robin and Emily had developed.

She rubbed her temples. Unfortunately, it was going to be difficult to dispel the rumors until their products actually launched, and even then, there would probably be speculation that they'd rapidly changed tack due to bad press. She and Robin had taken a hit, and her brother was right about one thing, they needed to get on top of the situation as soon as possible.

"I know. A few hours unplugged and everything goes to hell," Nick told an understandably upset Emily. "We'll issue a statement with some more information on the products in development. It won't completely halt the gossip, but it will at least be a sign that whatever was leaked was bogus."

"I just don't understand how this could have happened. I looked at what's online, and nothing in the proposals is anything Robin or I would have even suggested," she said, her voice sounding strained.

Nick bit his lip and looked up at Michelle sitting across from his desk. As always, she was perched on the edge of her chair as if she might need to flee any second. She raised her eyebrows and shrugged. She thought he should hold the small amount of information they had close to the vest until they had more time to assess the situation, and while it would be easier in the short term to play dumb, the long-term consequences of doing so weren't worth the immediate gain. Eventually, the truth was going to have to come out, so he thought he might as well control how that happened while he could.

He took a deep breath and said carefully, "They're old proposals from one of our in-house people. The reason we actually decided to go with outside talent for the line was that those initial proposals were so lackluster."

"Oh," Emily made an irritated noise. "So, how did they leak, and why is someone at Indulgence saying they came from Robin and me?"

"I wish I knew Emily." The fact that he had no idea where this was coming from or why it was leaking now scared him. He had thought he'd controlled the leaks when he'd fired Mae, but apparently someone in his company was either actively trying to hurt him or had a big mouth and bad information.

He promised her he'd call her as soon as he knew anything else and told her he'd see her later. He wanted to say more, but Michelle's presence limited his ability to speak freely.

As soon as he disconnected the call, he focused his full attention on Michelle. "We need to get control of this yesterday."

"We need a distraction."

"We've been over this. I want us to look above board to the public, to the press, to everyone. I don't want to play games. I want a statement that relates the details of the situation accurately without any spin, and I want this leak found and plugged."

Michelle paused before reminding him, "You know our sales have gone up since Michael Taliaferro has been headlining the gossip columns. Every time they feature him, they mention Indulgence. We could never afford that kind of publicity. It's increasing our national prominence without us having to do a thing." She shot him a meaningful look. "And that impact is just on our regular lines. His products aren't even available yet."

Nick knew she was right in general. Any press that did not down and out paint their company as dishonest was good press, and Michael Taliaferro was providing a bonanza. "The problem is that the niche bloggers who are up in arms about this story aren't going to care about more Michael Taliaferro gossip," he reminded her.

"True, but it will draw mainstream attention. We obviously do want to court the people who subscribe to Gluten-Free Life, but I don't see why we can't win over both groups," she countered. "For the Sweet Life base, we'll issue a carefully crafted statement and we'll release high-quality samples from the actual line to some influential bloggers. We'll also provide those bloggers with access to Emily and Robin." She took a breath and continued, "The readers of Clearinghouse News though, need something else to distract them and maintain their interest in us. I can't see anything more effective than a steady trickle of juicy celebrity gossip."

Nick knew she was right, but something in him rebelled at the cold-bloodedness of it. Maybe, he was going soft, but releasing gossip about Michael Taliaferro when the man wanted the situation kept as private as possible was a bridge he wasn't willing to cross. "Your analysis is right on," he told her. "But, we're not leaking anything about Taliaferro even if it might benefit us. That's a place I just won't go. He's part of this company, and I'm not going to make his life harder than it already is."

Michelle gave him an irritated look but said nothing. He knew she was unhappy with the way he was handling things, but he knew his way was the right way to go in the long run and he was the boss.

Plus, he did respect Taliaferro's need for privacy and had ethical problems with leaking the story, Emily had also factored heavily into his decision-making process. He knew that if he did decide to go against his better nature and sacrifice Michael's privacy for profit and she found out about it, she'd leave him. And that frightened him.

Chapter 20

"You were right," Robin said. Emily noted with alarm that her friend was close to tears.

"About what?" Emily asked cautiously. They were sitting in the small office in the back of the bakery with Emily seated at the desk and Robin draped on the couch.

Robin continued glumly, "I thought this deal was the best thing that could have happened to us, and I never even considered it could actually make things worse. I should have listened to you."

Emily sighed. Robin had had a hard time of it since the leaked information had hit the web. Because Emily had had appointments at the rehab center that she hadn't been able to reschedule, her partner had been shouldering the lion's share of managing their current PR disaster. Between keeping on top of the regular day-to-day needs of the bakery, coordinating with Indulgence's PR people and fielding inquiries from their clients and followers, she had been run ragged. If all that pressure weren't enough, she had been getting well-meaning but contradictory advice from old cooking school friends and restaurant colleagues. Emily had been trying to pitch in, but she obviously hadn't been doing enough.

"No," she assured her partner. "You were right. We needed the money too badly to be picky. This is a setback, but it's not the end of the world. Once our actual product hits the market, no one will even remember this little hiccup."

Robin gave her a suspicious look. "When did you turn into Polyanna?"

"I didn't. It's just that I've been letting you take on too much of this crap. From now on, I'm going to do a lot more to help."

Robin shook her head. "That's not it. Well, that's not entirely it." She took a shaky breath. "I want to believe this can still work, but you haven't been talking to these people. I think half of our potential customer base considers us sell outs right now. We're pretty much being completely dismissed on all of the influential blogs, so people in the community who don't know us personally are going to have a hard time trusting any product we offer."

"We'll work it out Robin. This isn't perfect, but at this point we need to make it work. What else are we going to do?"

Robin shifted uncomfortably and instead of answering Emily's question asked one of her own, "Em, have you checked your email lately or looked at Twitter?"

Emily nodded grimly.

"No matter what we do, we're going to have a hard time getting anyone to take us seriously."

Emily got up and went to sit next to Robin on the couch. She sat against the opposite arm and faced her friend, "We'll get through it Robin. Nick's looking for the leak and he has his people handling the fallout."

Robin squirmed uncomfortably and avoided Emily's gaze. "Greg says we should consider our options," she said.

"What does that mean?" Emily asked.

Robin took a deep breath. "He doesn't think we can back out over this incident, but he thinks we should document everything from here on out. Because if something like this happens again, Indulgence might rather settle with us and let us sever our relationship with the company than deal with an ugly public fight."

"Oh," Emily said taken aback. "Doesn't that seem pretty drastic?"

"He doesn't think we should try to storm out now, but we do need to keep our options open."

Emily felt blindsided. This situation seemed to be spiraling out of control, and she wasn't sure how to get a handle on it. "Wow, I did not see that coming," she said because she couldn't think of anything else to say.

"Really?" Robin asked sounding surprised. "Isn't this what you've been saying from the beginning of this whole thing?"

"Yeah, but you said I was being dramatic, and you were right. I think now that this is just getting blown out of proportion."

Robin shifted, and her eyes narrowed. "Out of proportion? I had to practically talk you off the ledge when you found out we were just going to have to work with Michael Taliaferro. Now, we're linked with some pretty bad gossip, and we've had our professional integrity questioned, and you think I'm blowing things out of proportion?"

Emily took a deep breath. "No, I just think maybe we need to see how this plays out before we make any rash decisions."

"Nice," Robin said, and Emily guessed that maybe, "rash" hadn't been the best word to choose. "That's a big change in a short time. Nick must be really great in bed."

Emily felt as if Robin had slapped her. Actually, she'd have preferred a slap. "That's not fair," she said trying to keep her voice steady.

Robin sighed. "I'm sorry Em." Her eyes teared. "Lately, I go straight to bitchy. Look, I get it okay. He's a great boyfriend, but we can't trust our careers to that." Before Emily could respond, she continued, "I'm not saying we do anything crazy. We just have to make sure we look out for ourselves first and Indulgence second."

Finding Love in the Sweet Life

Emily was trying not to cry. "I never said we shouldn't look out for ourselves. I just think we should give it time."

Robin shook her head. "Emily, let's please be real here and not think that Nick Hawkins isn't looking out for himself above all because he definitely is, and you know it deep down. If it's a choice between us and his profit margin, he's going to throw us under the bus in a heart beat."

Emily wanted to scream. She had not expected this. "I'm glad you think I've gone completely brainless over a man," she said unable to disguise the hurt in her voice. She got up and paced back to the desk. Right now, she wanted a buffer between her and Robin.

"That's not what I said Emily and that's not what I meant." Robin sounded exhausted.

Emily felt like demanding Robin tell her just exactly what she'd meant then, but she thought that if Robin answered that question in her current state of mind, their relationship would never recover. Instead, she said, "Look I don't want to fight. I'll just talk to you later okay. I think we both need to cool down."

She expected Robin to protest, but she just nodded sadly. Emily swallowed back a sob and gathered her things. She had to get out of her before she lost it. Breaking down was not going to help the situation right now.

"I need a favor," Michael's voice came through her speakerphone. She was on her way home from the bakery, and after her conversation with Robin she didn't really have the energy for Michael's usual games. Really, she just wanted to take a hot bath and have a good long cry before she had to deal with any more crap.

"You sound like you're standing at the bottom of a lake," Emily told him. Even taking into account the fact that he was on speakerphone, the echo was bad.

"I'm on the stairs to the Speedline tunnel. I was down on the platform, but the signal's crap down there."

"Why are you on the Speedline platform?"

"That's where the favor comes in. I need you to pick me up," he said. He sounded almost as tired as she felt.

"What happened to your rental?" she asked. Sometimes, Michael took the Speedline if he wanted to drink and get back to his hotel in the same night, but if he planned to crash at her place or wasn't going to drink, it was easier for him to drive his rental car than to mess with trains.

"I turned it in. I'll get a new one tomorrow." Even with the weird echoes, he really did sound like crap.

"Michael, I have had the worst day on record, and I don't want to play 20 questions," she said trying not to snap at him. "Please, please just tell me what's going on without making me drag it out of you in teeny tiny bits."

"Alright." She heard him take a breath, and she braced herself for something insane. "So, apparently, some gossip columnist got hold of the story about my fight with Selena's man and someone's cellphone picture of my screwed-up face is now online. I guess even a minor celebrity warrants major attention with enough sex and violence. Then when you add an NFL star, it really takes off."

"Oh," she actually could not form a single rational sentence in response to that.

"So anyway, I need to lay low, and I kinda need your help with that," he said in his most pathetic voice.

She sighed. "What do you need?" As she asked it, she resisted the urge to burst into hysterical laughter. If someone had told her two months ago that she'd not only be working with Michael Taliaferro but would also let him adopt her as some kind of substitute big sister, she'd have told them they were crazy.

"I ditched my rental since it was little conspicuous, and I really don't want to go back to my hotel, so I was hoping I could crash at your place for a couple of days," he said in his sad puppy voice.

"You want to stay with me?" Emily asked caught off guard.

"Yeah," he sounded unsure, which was new for him. "I mean if that's okay. Oh shit! I forgot. Is Hawkins there? I can find a hotel in Jersey. That's probably low key enough to wait this out."

"No, of course you can stay at my place," she said. It wasn't in her to let him stay by himself when he obviously needed a friend and she had a couch and a spare room open. "You're cooking, though, and you have to sleep in the spare room and no complaining about my cat."

She knew he was really low when he didn't respond with snark. "Sure. Thanks Em. I' should be in Woodcrest in about 20 minutes."

She agreed and disconnected the call. "So much for that hot bath," she muttered.

"Oh that feels amazing," Emily nearly purred. She was leaning back against Nick on his soft leather couch, and he was rubbing her shoulders. He really did have great hands.

"We aim to please," he whispered while massaging a knot she'd believed had taken up permanent residence right below her shoulder blade."

"You aim to get laid," she corrected laughing.

"That too," he agreed easily. "The getting laid has definitely been the high point of my week by a mile."

"Yeah it has," she agreed. "These leaks are just making everyone crazy and stressed. I just wish there was some news."

"I thought we agreed to ban work talk," he said. His hands stilled on her shoulders.

She and Nick had reached an agreement on Monday that they'd keep business talk away from their evenings together. She'd resisted at first because she needed someone to talk to about the situation, but eventually, she'd agreed that they both needed time away from all the business crap.

"We did," she turned and brushed a quick kiss on his hand. "I don't want to kill the mood, but it's important to us and we're both stressed about the situation."

"We both need a break," he said, starting to rub her shoulders again. "Plus we agreed to keep work and personal life separate. That's the only way this works."

She nodded hesitantly. They had agreed to that. She just wasn't sure it had been a good idea.

Finding Love in the Sweet Life

Today was Friday, and this was the third night they'd been able to steal together. The online furor had mostly died down after Emily and Robin had done some successful interviews with bloggers, and Nick's PR people had been quick to contradict rumors with facts. While she and Robin were still wary around one another, the positive press seemed to have calmed Robin's worst fears. It had been an exhausting few days, though, and she knew Nick was still beating himself up about the leak in his company he hadn't been able to find. He'd been working on it pretty much every second he hadn't been with her or sleeping. She just wished he'd talk to her about it.

"And your new roommate has made finding time alone even more of a challenge." He gave her shoulders a final squeeze and maneuvered them both around so that they faced one another.

She rolled her eyes. It was an obvious ploy to change the subject, but she let it go. This fight would keep.

"I thought you liked challenges," she said giving him a teasing grin.

"I do. I just don't like Michael Taliaferro in your apartment," he said frankly.

She started to laugh, but his eyes told her he was serious, so she settled for rolling her eyes. "You're jealous? Of Michael?"

"Not jealous exactly," he conceded. "I just don't like the idea of him staying there alone with you."

She shook her head in disbelief. "I think I can protect my virtue from big bad Michael Taliaferro."

"I never said…" He trailed off and sighed. "Look, I'm sorry. I'm tired. I shouldn't have said anything about it. I trust you. Hell, I even trust him with you. It's just that logic and instinct sometimes don't agree." He shrugged helplessly.

"I should be offended, but I'll give you a pass because of the fabulous massage and the fact that you realized your mistake," she said snuggling closer to him.

"Also, you want to use me for my body," she murmured.

"Well that too." He pulled her even closer, and she went eagerly, settling herself on his lap.

He kissed her neck and she bit back a whimper. She felt his hot mouth blaze a path to her ear and couldn't help jumping a little when he lightly bit her earlobe.

She felt him moan against her ear as she squirmed on his lap. "Then," he whispered into her ear. "Right now would be a good time."

And for a while, she forgot about roommates and best friends and leaked information and angry bloggers. Even with the distraction, she couldn't shake the sense that this was all just a little too good to be true.

Chapter 21

"I don't blame him for it. Hell, I'd have probably done the same thing, but he's still a son of a bitch." Michael took a bite of his macaroni and cheese. He was sprawled at her tiny kitchen table. His trademark stubble was less carefully maintained than usual, and his hair had crossed the line from artfully mussed to just messy. Even so, He could have incited a riot just by walking through a roomful of women. Emily was still completely unmoved.

"We're not talking about this again. He didn't leak it. I told you. He told you." She put the last pot into the dishwasher and sat down across from him.

"Eat your food before it gets cold," he told her.

She rolled her eyes at him. His change of subject signaled that he was as sick of the topic as she was. Since he'd moved in to her place over a week ago, he had been insisting that Nick must have leaked the story about the fight to the press. She'd countered with the fact that other people also knew, and it wasn't like Michael hadn't looked like he'd been in a terrible fight. He refused to believe the leak was coincidence and to make matters worse, he'd convinced Robin and Mia of the fact.

Emily shook her head. She still couldn't get over how quickly Michael had turned Mia from homicidal to nearly tolerant. He really did have the ability to grow on people. He was kind of like fungus that way. Oh, Mia still rambled on about hating him, but there was a lot less rancor in it since they'd spent some time together.

She took a bite of her mac and cheese. "Oh wow," she couldn't help saying. "This is freaking amazing. The one perk of living with a chef is the amazing quality of comfort food. Any other roommate would have made boxed and called it a night."

He shuddered in exaggerated horror. "You're lucky you have me then."

"You leave your crap around and never do dishes. You're lucky you can cook." She took another bite, closed her eyes in brief ecstasy and then added, "And that you're reasonably decorative."

He grinned at her, but then, the expression faded. "I should go back to Chicago," he said. "I don't really need to be here for development anymore. The press stuff is pretty minimal and we could probably arrange some distance stuff."

"Why haven't you?" she asked and then realized it sounded harsh. It was just that she'd been wondering for a while. "I don't mean I want you to leave. It just hasn't been the best trip for you so far."

He shrugged. "I want to see something through for once, be really hands on. Plus, it hasn't really been that bad."

She thought about pointing out that he'd been beaten up and had his name and face plastered all over gossip sites. That was probably pretty normal for him though. She guessed that his admission was probably as close as he'd come to saying he liked staying with her.

She smiled at him. "You can stay for as long as you want."

He grinned back at her like a kid who'd been told he'd done a good job. Somehow, Michael Taliaferro had become her adopted baby brother. She wanted to shake her head at the sheer impossibility of it, but she was pretty sure he'd take it the wrong way.

His smile faded, and he gave her an uncertain look before he confessed, "I got an offer to open a new restaurant in Center City and I just might take it."

She blinked at him stunned. He'd never even let on that something like that was in the works, and it wasn't like Philadelphia had been especially kind to him so far.

When she didn't immediately respond, he rushed on nervously, "I mean I'll get my own place, obviously. I like your couch and all and I'm even getting used to your cat, but I need space."

Before she could form some kind of response to that, her phone went off.

"Lover boy?" he asked, rolling his eyes.

She looked down and shook her head. "Robin," she told him.

She took the call. Things between them might still be a little weird, but they were working on patching them up. And since they had a business to run together and a tasting event to plan for next week, they didn't really have time to indulge any hurt feelings.

After hours in his office at Indulgence, Nick stared at his laptop and felt his stomach drop. He'd tried to organize everything they had on the source of the old leaked memos and the gossip about Michael. It wasn't much, but if you read between the lines, there were clues. He just really didn't like where those clues were pointing.

For a moment, he wished he'd worked on his speech for an upcoming industry conference. That was what he'd intended to do when he'd learned Emily had had to meet with Robin tonight, and he'd have time on his hands. He just hadn't been able to focus on the task at hand. His relationship with Emily was becoming strained and he knew it was these damned leaks driving a wedge between them, so he'd decided to see another look would help solve the mystery.

Michelle had suggested two separate sources and that was still a possibility. She'd tried to convince him the news about Michael had come from outside the company and the bogus recipes and information had come from within. He wished that was true, but there was one person at Indulgence with the access and motivation to leak all of the information that had gotten out so far. He'd just never believed she'd do it to him.

Thinking back though, it made a sick kind of sense. Michelle had been very adamant in her belief that gossip about Michael helped their bottom line, and she'd been the first one he'd called when Michael had walked into Emily's apartment after his fight. That leak he could almost understand. Oh, he was still furious at the thought she could do it after he'd been crystal clear that he wanted the information kept confidential, but he did understand it. She was almost as fanatically devoted to Indulgence as he was, and he'd believed she was helping to save the company she loved.

The leak that made less sense was the one involving the bogus information and recipes because that leak hurt the company and had the potential to kill a line into which they'd already invested quite a bit of time and money.

Maybe, he was wrong about the whole thing, jumping at shadows. He just couldn't forget the fact that Michelle had never wanted to deal with unknowns like Robin and Emily. Maybe, she thought the company would be better off if they killed the deal and focused on Taliaferro's line exclusively? It just didn't make a lot of sense, and because it didn't make sense and he lacked actual hard evidence, there wasn't much he could do but wait, watch her and hope she slipped up or he discovered the leak had come from someone else. He sighed. He really hoped he was wrong.

He adjusted his shirt collar, feeling like he was being strangled. He brushed his knuckle almost involuntarily over that spot under his left collarbone that had become a kind of touchstone, a reminder to keep pushing and take what he wanted. The problem was that no matter what he did he felt like everything he wanted was about to slip through his fingers. Even his relationship with Emily felt tenuous lately. When she didn't think he was looking, she'd give him looks that held such doubt that it nearly broke his heart.

He ran his hand through his hair, closed his eyes and counted to ten. He needed to get it together. All this doubt and worry was not him, and he needed to be the hyper-focused, deal-closing Nick if he wanted any hope of hanging on to those things that mattered most to him.

When he slept, he looked younger, more carefree. She supposed everyone did, but when Nick Hawkins was awake he looked in control, gorgeous and slightly dangerous. He was intimidating as hell, and even when he was relaxed, there was always a part of him that seemed on edge. Now, asleep, that part was still. She brushed her hand over his wavy sun-kissed hair, careful not to wake him. It had been a tough week, and he needed sleep. Everyone was on his case from bloggers to the press to his contractors.

She sighed and looked away. When she looked at him, all sense left her head, and she needed to focus. Robin was getting more and more uneasy. She and Greg thought they could put enough pressure on Nick to get out of part of the deal and still keep the bakery open.

A few months ago, she would have jumped at the chance to run far from the corporate world because she hadn't trusted big companies, and she'd worried that she and Robin would be considered nothing but shills since neither of them were particularly well known. Now, she wasn't sure. She liked the idea of bringing their food to a wider audience and she just didn't believe, didn't want to believe Nick had been planning to screw them over from the outset. Because if she believed that, she'd have to believe the man she was in love with didn't really exist and that she was sleeping with a man she didn't know at all.

She carefully got out of bed. He gave a small moan and moved restlessly but didn't wake. She moved to the dresser and got a t-shirt out of the drawer he'd cleared for her and pulled it over her head before moving to the window. She looked out at the city and marveled at how she'd ended up here of all places with Nick Hawkins of all men. They'd been dating for months and sleeping together for weeks, but she still felt like a part of him, a big part was still hidden from her, and it scared her. Sometimes, she'd catch him looking at her oddly like he was trying to solve a puzzle. Sometimes, she was flattered. She liked the idea of being a woman of mystery. More and more though, it made her feel uneasy. Was she a deal he was looking to close? Was he deciding what to tell her and what secrets he needed to keep?

Emily rubbed a hand over her face. The anxiety was eating her up. She'd been supportive, keeping business out their relationship as they'd agreed to do, but every day it got harder and harder. Robin was pressuring her for more information, for a decision. Michael refused to talk about it, but she felt it between them. With Nick, there were uncomfortable silences and lots of passionate sex. It was as if they were both afraid to talk, afraid the wrong word would break the spell. She knew she'd been overcompensating by being too supportive and he'd responded by being unnaturally upbeat.

She bit her lip. Something had to give and soon. This compartmentalization was ripping her apart, but when she'd casually floated the idea of going a little more public at work, he'd nixed it. Oh, he said it was her choice, but he'd made it abundantly clear that he didn't think it was a good time. The secrecy had been fun at first, but pretending distance was getting to her. Much as she wished they could just go on ignoring the situation until they had real answers, that didn't seem practical any longer. They were going to have to talk about it, and when they talked about it, she very much feared the little bubble of happiness they had made was going to burst. Then she would nursing another broken heart.

Chapter 22

"We're just thrilled to be able to bring our food to a wider audience," Emily told the woman in front of her. She thought her name was Julie, but she'd met so many people today that it was possible the last one had been Julie. She did remember that Maybe-Julie ran a popular blog for people with Celiac disease because she'd asked a lot about the gluten-free options that would be available and had complimented Emily on the gluten-free carrot cake she'd sampled. "Giving people with special needs the option to enjoy the same type of gourmet products as everyone else is important to us," she added.

"Aren't you concerned about quality control with all of the leaks?" Maybe-Julie pressed.

Inside, Emily wanted to scream. The bakery was stuffy and crowded, and her head was pounding. She'd been giving the same practiced responses for hours, and she just wanted to go somewhere cool and quiet. Robin had bowed out 45 minutes ago. As her pregnancy had progressed, she'd developed sciatica. That meant she had a tough time standing for any length of time, so Emily had to pick up the slack. Keeping that in mind, she smiled at woman in front of her instead of snapping. She needed to be tactful and professional.

"We have every faith that the problem has been addressed and that the leaked recipes were nothing more than early concepts that were never meant to see the light of day." Emily told the woman who she was starting to think might not actually be named Julie after all. She forced a laugh. "Really, we're grateful they were so bad because otherwise Indulgence wouldn't have needed to bring us on board."

The brunette whose name she had obviously forgotten opened her mouth to say something else, but before she could speak, a voice from behind Emily cut her off, "So, you aren't concerned at all with Nick Hawkins' attitude toward you and your partner? You don't think his dismissiveness could compromise your ability to advocate for the quality you've promised?"

Emily tensed and turned to face a tall woman with dark hair and narrow black eyes. She recognized her as Kate Fields, a local food columnist Nick had introduced her to at another event. She had a reputation for being extremely difficult and for making snap judgements. Common sense said that once Kate decided she didn't like you, you had two choices: deal with the constant negative press or move on. Emily had looked for her earlier, but she hadn't seen her. She'd thought that this event was probably too boring for a woman who fancied herself a top food journalist. Apparently, Kate had decided to come slumming.

Emily swallowed. "I don't think Mr. Hawkins or anyone from Indulgence has been dismissive of us, Kate. They've actually been extremely supportive and we've been impressed with their commitment to quality." She was mildly disturbed at how easily the practiced answers came to her lips now.

"So, you've seen the emails on Clearinghouse News and you aren't concerned?" Kate pressed.

Emily sighed. Would they never stop asking the same questions? She'd naively hoped that once everyone tasted the real food and got a look at the actual nutrition information that everything would blow over. Despite the fact that the food had been an unqualified success, the questions persisted. People loved a scandal and were hesitant to let one, even a small and silly one, go easily. She forced a smile, and said, "Yes, as you can see, that report was very outdated and did not reflect any of the products Robin and I actually developed."

"No, I mean the new emails, the ones that leaked this morning," she clarified in a tone of barely suppressed delight. She made no effort to keep her voice conversational. Emily wouldn't be surprised if people on the street out front had heard that announcement.

It seemed as if all the conversations around Emily stopped as around her, guests turned to see what was going on. Emily felt like a bug pinned to a card. "I'm afraid I'm not sure to what you're referring then," she said, her voice tight but even.

Kate's face bore what might have been a try at a sympathetic expression, but it was ruined by the anticipation burning in her eyes. "I'm sorry. I guess you were too consumed with party preparations to notice them. They're internal emails between Nick Hawkins and Michelle Paul about getting relative unknowns with solid credentials for the new diet line because the credentials would placate the…" she stopped and looked at her phone "'lunatic fringe of the food blog world,' but unknowns would be easy to control and wouldn't insist on expensive and impossible things."

Emily opened her mouth, but she couldn't form words.

When she didn't immediately respond, Kate pressed, "Things like the kind of quality control you've been promising everyone since they brought you on board."

She felt like someone had just punched her in the stomach, but she had to say something. She forced herself to speak. "I'm afraid I'm not familiar with these emails and I can't comment until I've looked at them."

Emily was pretty proud that she'd managed a semi-coherent statement without her voice breaking when inside she was raw. If the emails said what Kate said they did, it pretty much confirmed what she'd thought when Indulgence first offered to do business with Sweet Life. Somehow, though, after all the rest of the leaks and all that had gone before hearing the feared truth from the mouth of this smug reporter was just more than she could deal with.

"I'm sorry, but you'll have to excuse Ms. McCauley," Nick said coming up behind her. She really didn't want to see him right now, but since he was her best hope for getting out of this uncomfortable situation, she'd get over it. She'd noticed him leave to take a phone call in the back a few minutes ago. Now, she was pretty sure she knew what it had been about

"Mr. Hawkins, do you have a comment about the emails Clearinghouse has obtained?" Kate asked turning to Nick.

Nick took Emily's arm. "I'm sorry Ms. Fields. We'll make a statement later. For now, I'll just say that we have the utmost respect for Ms. McCauley and Ms. Mead, and the new Guiltless Indulgence line they have created for us is of the highest quality."

Emily was vaguely aware of Kate and some of the others following them and shouting questions as Nick pulled her into the back and shut the door.

"I want to go home," Emily said from the passenger seat.

Nick had had one of his employees bring his car to the back of the bakery and had pulled out before Kate and the others could descend on them. Emily hadn't said much through the process. He wasn't sure if she was shocked, angry, sad or a combination of all of those emotions. His own stomach churned. God, what a stupid mess this had turned into.

The tasting had been going quite well. Emily and Robin had really won over all of the carefully chosen guests and Emily had seemed to relax into the role of spokesperson, a position he knew she found uncomfortable and he had been so damn proud of her. At first, he'd ignored Michelle's repeated calls, but when she'd texted him 911, he'd gone to the back and heard about the latest leaked emails. Unfortunately, he hadn't been able to get to Emily before Kate sprung the news on her in that very public setting.

"Why don't we go to my place?" he asked, He didn't want to take her home where she could kick him out. They needed to talk, and he wanted his say before she kicked him to the curb.

"Nick," she said in a pained voice that held absolute conviction, "if you don't turn to take me home, I will jump out of this car and walk."

"Okay, whatever you want." Maybe, now wasn't the time to push her.

She was silent for the rest of the drive.

When they'd reached her apartment, he'd told Taliaferro to get lost. At first the other man had seemed on the verge of telling him to go to hell, but with a look from Emily, he'd gone. He had, however, informed them he'd be back in an hour and that if Emily texted him, he'd be there in minutes. In other circumstances, Nick might have been amused at big, bad Michael Taliaferro transforming into an overprotective brother.

Emily had ignored their posturing and gone to change. He'd thought better of following her into the bedroom.

When she came out dressed in yoga pants and a tank top her hair in a ponytail, he stood. She ignored him and crossed to the overstuffed chair across from the couch. He sat back down.

"Em, those emails weren't even really about you and Robin, and we didn't intend to trick anyone. They were just....."

"Business," she asked impatiently. "I'm not an idiot. I knew why you wanted Robin and me."

"That's not exactly true."

She shook her head and continued as if he hadn't spoken. "You wanted people you thought would be beholden to you and we knew that."

He looked at her in confusion. He'd expected her to rail at him to call him names, and he'd dreaded the prospect. As it turned out, this calm understanding was far worse.

"But you also promised not to ruin our reputations, and all of this makes us look bad, makes us look like gullible fools." Her voice shook a little.

"Em, I'm sorry," he started.

She shook her head and cut him off before he could say anything else. "You wanted this thing compartmentalized and I thought that's what I wanted too, but..." her voice started to break.

He moved toward her, but she held up a hand to ward him off.

"I can't do this. I can't be your girlfriend and then go react like I'm supposed to when crap like this comes out." She laughed, but there was no humor in it. "I'm not mad about the stupid emails. I'm mad because I'm in this shitty position, because I let myself get in this shitty position."

"What position?" he asked. His head hurt. He felt like he'd stepped in quicksand. They apparently weren't having the fight he'd thought they'd have.

The look she shot him made him doubt his intelligence.

"The position where I am a doormat," she snapped. "I told you how it was with Pete, and I know this isn't the same, but something about it feels like the same, like I'm just supposed to be along for the ride." She made a frustrated noise and continued, "I have no credibility because of the leaks. My business partner is pissed at me because I'm with you and we don't even have a real public relationship. Does it sound like I'm in a good position to you?" She laughed bitterly.

"Em, I don't want you in a bad position. This is probably a bad time to take our relationship public because of the optics, but we can come up with a plan and...."

He trailed off when he registered the expression on her face. She looked like she couldn't decide whether to laugh, cry or go for his throat. He swallowed the rest of what he'd intended to say.

"Don't bother," she sounded exhausted. "I wouldn't want to complicate things." Her tone was bitter. She scrubbed her hand over her face. "God, I'm such an idiot."

"Emily," he tried again.

"Are you the leak Nick?" she asked him before he could say anything more.

He felt like she'd slapped him. "Are you seriously asking me that?"

She shrugged. "All of this stuff has been off limits, and now, I'm wondering exactly how much of an idiot I've been. Michael and Robin told me you were the leak or knew who was. I didn't want to believe them, but I need to know." Her voice was shaky.

He felt his temper flare. "Why in the hell would I leak those emails. They hurt Indulgence as much as they hurt you and Robin."

"Not the emails and not the recipes either," she said, shaking her head. "I mean Michael's fight. He told me you leaked it to draw attention from the recipes, and I told him he was crazy. Robin, Mia, my brother all tried to tell me you did it, but I said you wouldn't."

"No, I didn't leak it," his voice was tense with anger and hurt.

"Do you know who did?" she asked, but from her tone, he thought she had the same suspicions he did because that information about Michael had been too conveniently timed not to have come from inside the company.

"Emily. I honestly don't know who leaked it," he said even though he was pretty sure he did know.

She gave him a sad look. "And you don't want to know."

He shifted uncomfortably. She knew him better than he'd thought. "If you want me to ask Michelle about it, I will."

She shook her head sadly. "It's too late Nick. I just can't do it anymore. I can't compartmentalize and hold everything in because I'm too scared to destroy something that might not be worth saving, something I'm not even sure is real."

He felt like she'd kicked him in the stomach. "You don't mean that Emily. My God, you know it's business, that it has nothing to do with our personal relationship."

"Yeah, because the optics would suck if we mixed the two," her wide green eyes, shiny with unshed tears, met his. "But I can't do this separation thing anymore, optics or not. I can't pigeonhole my life, tiptoe around work issues because my boyfriend is also my boss, and I sure as hell can't keep my mouth shut around the man I'm working for when he tries to screw over my partner and me because he happens to be my boyfriend."

"Em please," he tried to think, tried to form words to convince her she was wrong that he hadn't expected her to keep everything neatly separated, hadn't wanted her to keep her mouth shut, but a part of him knew that would be a lie. He'd always been able to say whatever was needed to close a deal, but in that moment, the thought of using such tactics with this woman seemed an unspeakable profanity.

"Nick," the tears running down her face nearly broke him. "I can't do it not like this. I thought I could. I said I could, and I'm sorry for that."

Part of him hoped that he could seduce her out of the idea, that he could make grand promises and make her believe him, so they could go back to whatever they'd had. Unfortunately, she was right. What they'd had was based on his need to keep her in a box, so instead of making promises he never could keep, he said, "I'm not done fighting for you Em."

As he left, he heard her crying softly and it took all he had not to go back to her.

Chapter 23

Nick stared at the drink in his hand. Why had he left her like that? He knew he could have talked her around. If she'd been any other woman, he'd have done it, but something about her, how he was with her had made him lose his edge. And, she'd hurt him too. Her accusations had hit a little too close to home, made him see himself a little more clearly than he wanted. For the first time in a long time, he'd felt helpless.

He took a drink of his gin and tonic and enjoyed the burn as the alcohol worked down his throat. His hand brushed over the familiar spot just below his left collarbone. The tattoo had become kind of a touchstone, a way to remind himself why he had to push so hard. Today, he let himself remember the time before he'd needed that kind of reminder.

His father hadn't been much older than he was now when he'd died. A drunk driver had ended the carefree part of Nick's childhood; a phone call in the middle of the night had announced it. He'd spent more than a decade trying to forget the sound of the scream his mother had let out after she'd answered that call.

His dad had had big dreams. Nick could still remember his talk of a bright future when they'd have plenty of money and could go exciting places, like Disney World, Europe and The Islands. Those tales had been Nick's bedtime stories and in the end, that's all they'd been. His dad had been a dreamer not a doer, and he'd left so much that he'd promised still undone when he died. That thought had haunted Nick, and he'd vowed the same would never be said of him. At age 16, trying to comfort his distraught mother, he'd felt helpless, hopeless, and he'd been running from that feeling for the entirety of his adult life.

Nick downed the rest of his drink in one gulp and looked out on his very expensive view. There had to be a way out of this, a way to keep Emily without damaging Indulgence. He wanted the woman and the success, and he couldn't accept that there wasn't a way to get exactly what he wanted.

"I found our leak," Michelle announced. Three days after his fight with Emily, Nick was having trouble focusing. He knew he hadn't been particularly productive or pleasant to be around, but Michelle's words gave him hope. If she'd found the leak, he could get the company back on track. He could show Emily that he had it together and that they could be an official couple. He could get her back.

"Who is it?" he asked.

Michelle looked sad for a moment. "Joe," she said in an uncharacteristically soft tone.

"What? Are you sure?" Nick asked. She had to be mistaken. "Why would he do that? We just gave him a giant promotion. He's pretty much running one of our new lines." As much as he wanted to find the leak, he couldn't believe that it could be Joe.

Michelle sat in one of the chairs facing his desk. She looked unusually tired. "He didn't do it on purpose. At least, I don't think he did." She stopped to take a deep breath. "I think his girlfriend is the leak."

"But, these leaks were documents not just information," Nick reminded her. "The first Taliaferro leak I could see, but the others included internal Indulgence documents, so had to have been a direct insider."

"It's a former insider with access to Joe's computer," she said. "Nick, it's Mae."

"What?" Nick asked. He'd fired Mae Hough for the damage she'd done to Indulgence. She'd been publicly bad mouthing him ever since, but he'd never considered she could be the one behind their current troubles. "How is that possible? She and Joe are together? How did we not know this?"

"They were really good at keeping things quiet," Michelle said. "At first, it was because of company policy and after we fired her, he didn't think it would be good for his career if anyone knew they were an item. I only found out because my assistant came to me with some old gossip. She didn't actually believe it, but she thought I should know it was out there." She sighed. "They've been together since before we fired Mae."

"You're sure?" he hadn't expected this. Joe. He just couldn't get his head around it.

She nodded, "He confirmed it just now. I don't think he knew about the leaks at first. They were actually too tame for what he expected from Mae, but she's smart. She wanted to chip away at us, have us chase our tails for a while, and she didn't want Joe to know it was her. He's suspected for a while, but he's only known for sure for a few days. He claims he's been trying to figure out a way to come clean. "

"Why isn't he telling me this himself?"

"I thought it would be better if I told you before you talked to him." She gave him a concerned look. "You've been off lately and I wanted to make sure you didn't do anything rash like fire him."

"Of course I'm going to fire him," Nick said looking at Michelle in disbelief. "His carelessness has cost us time and money and hurt our reputation."

"But firing him hurts us more," she said. "There's too much attention on us right now. If we fire Joe, there will be rumors and speculation, and we'll have someone else out there with a potential grudge against us in possession of inside information."

It went against his instincts, but he knew Michelle made sense. "So what do you want to do?"

"Let him resign in a few weeks. He'll take leave until then and quietly slip away. He's even offered to resign."

Nick sighed. This whole thing went against his nature, but Michelle was right. Firing Joe with the way things stood would be a disaster right now.

"Okay, let's go talk to him," he said.

Michelle took a deep breath as if she needed to steel herself for a difficult task. "Before we do that, there's something else you should know." She gave him an inscrutable look. "Although, I think you already know."

Nick nodded. Today was apparently his day for being punched in the gut. "I really hoped I was wrong," he told her.

The furniture was dusty. Unopened mail was strewn on the coffee table. Her laundry hamper overflowed, and the state of her bathroom should not be discussed in polite company. Her roommate didn't seem to mind, but as far as she could tell, as long as the kitchen was clean. Michael wouldn't notice if he were living in an actual garbage dump.

She knew she should get off the couch and do something, but as it was, she could barely even motivate herself to shower and go to work. The phone rang. She'd call whoever it was back later. It was probably Robin anyway. They were supposed to talk about hiring someone to represent their interests. Neither of them was ready to back out of the Indulgence deal even if it was possible, but having dedicated representation would help protect their reputations.

She should answer the call, but she wasn't sure she could take more fussing today. After she'd told her friend that she'd broken up with Nick, Robin had gone all mother hen on her. Emily was really glad they weren't fighting anymore, but all of the concerned looks and questions made her feel smothered. She tried to be polite and she loved Robin for caring so much, but it just made her feel worse than she already did.

"We're going out," Michael announced as he pushed into the apartment.

"I'm not," she told him. His version of comfort seemed to consist of bullying her into doing things, but that's not what she wanted either. Really, she wanted Nick back, but she'd always wanted things that weren't good for her.

The painful fact was she'd been stupid enough to fall in love again with a man who could never put her first. Nick was a great boyfriend as long as she stayed in her compartment. With him, Indulgence came first, and it always would. For a lot of people, that might be okay, but she couldn't do it. She deserved better.

"Em, come on," he wheedled. "We'll go to a sports bar and watch the game. You can make fun of me for not knowing anything about baseball. It'll be fun. We'll even get Mia to come. She knows less about baseball than I do, so you can mock both of us."

She snorted. "Yeah, it'll be great until someone recognizes you. Then, it's even odds whether we get mobbed for autographs or I have to referee a fight."

He grinned at her. "But at least it will be a distraction."

She smiled. "Thanks. I just don't feel up to it tonight."

Really, she just wanted to be alone, but his hurt look had her saying, "But maybe we could stay in, get take out and watch the game."

Before he could respond, the buzzer sounded. Michael got up to answer it, and she heard Nick ask to come up.

"Not a good time Hawkins," Michael said in a flat voice.

The cowardly part of Emily wanted to curl into the couch and let Michael handle it, but she couldn't do that. Even without all of the personal baggage, they were in business together, and she needed to be a grown up.

She sighed and said, "Let him up, Michael."

Nick was getting sick of Michael Taliaferro answering Emily's door, but he guessed he wasn't in a position to complain right now. Nick knew Taliaferro was working on his sauce line, doing publicity and in talks to run a local restaurant, but he seemed to be underfoot a lot.

When he'd told them the source of the leaks, both Emily and Michael had been surprised, but they'd agreed with his decision to let those responsible resign. The bad publicity from more public firings would hurt all of them.

Taliaferro had left to run some errands, but he'd announced he wouldn't be long with a meaningful look at Nick. Now, alone with Emily, Nick wasn't sure how to start. He opened his mouth to say something, but quickly shut it when she spoke first.

"I'm sorry about Michelle," she said with a concerned look. "I know she's been with you for a long time."

His first instinct was to wave off the concern, but he thought better of it. "Yeah. I actually wanted to find a way for her to stay, but she leaked information to a reporter after I told her not to do it, so there was just no way I could ever trust her again." He shook his head sadly. "I know she did it for the company, but we just can't work together after that."

Emily nodded. "And as mad as I am about the leaks, I feel bad for Joe too," she said. "It was all a big stupid mess."

"Yeah," he said and laughed humorlessly. He was grateful that Emily hadn't pointed out that in some sense, this giant mess had resulted from the same kind of secret relationship he'd tried to push her into.

"Thanks for coming out here to tell me." She smiled wanly. "I'm sure Robin will be relieved too. I should probably call her."

Nick swallowed. He knew a dismissal when he heard one, but he wasn't ready to go. "Emily, now that this is over, do you think we could try again?" Before she could respond, he held up a hand and added, "No secrets this time."

For a moment, he thought she was going to nod, but she seemed to shake herself before she took a deep breath and said, "I don't know. I'm not trying to be coy, but I just don't think it's going to work and it's not because I don't love you," she told him with tears in her eyes. "Your company comes first and I do believe you care about me and want to try, but I also think that you're going to break my heart."

"That's not fair," he said, and he couldn't keep the anger and hurt from his voice. He knew he'd kept her at more of a distance than she'd wanted, but he'd let her in farther than anyone else.

Finding Love in the Sweet Life

She watched him for what seemed like hours but was probably only a few seconds. It was as if she was expecting something from him. Unfortunately, his mind was a blank. He was going to fail. She was going to turn him away, and he had no idea how to fix it. He felt like he couldn't breathe. His mind raced.

She sighed. "I'm tired, Nick. I just want to sleep for a while. We have all that publicity stuff this week and I really just need time."

In the end, he took the hint, and he left her again. For the first time in memory, he'd failed to close the deal and he didn't even have a ready back-up plan.

Chapter 24

"You're drunk," Nick said.

Taliaferro smiled at him. It was a dopey, drunken grin. "You're drunker," the other man slurred.

Nick shrugged and put his hand to his face when the room started to spin a little. Maybe, he was drunker than he'd thought. "But it's my booze," he said as if that explained everything.

Taliaferro nodded. "Yeah, it's the good stuff too. I wish you hadn't dragged me out of the bar though. I think that redhead was into me."

Nick rolled his eyes, "You were about to get beat up by the guy she was with."

On his way out of Emily's, Nick had run into Michael who had taken one look at him and announced that he needed to get wasted. Nick initiallly protested. He didn't even really like Michael Taliaferro, and he had no interest in going drinking with him, but the son of a bitch was persuasive. Plus, the thought of going home after the shit day he'd had hadn't been all that appealing. The next thing he'd known, they'd been in a bar. Then, when Taliaferro had looked to be on the verge of starting a fight, Nick had hauled him out of there. They'd ridden the Speedline to the city and had somehow found their way to Nick's apartment, which was fully stocked with booze.

Michael shrugged, "I could have taken him." He let out a contented sigh and took a swig of his drink. "I'm okay drinking all your booze instead." He laughed. "And sleeping on your couch. If I go back to Em's like this, she might murder me in my sleep."

The alcohol in Nick's stomach suddenly felt like acid. "She's good at that," he said.

"You're not good enough for her," Taliaferro announced.

Nick remembered something, something he hadn't fully registered sober and he grinned. "She loves me," he said. Then, he nodded. "She said it today." Well, that's not exactly what she'd said. It was kind of tangled up in his head, but she'd definitely used the word love.

"Oh yeah," Taliaferro asked and then shrugged. "Then, I'll let you have some free advice. Also, I'm drinking your booze, so I probably owe you or something."

"What's that?"

"Grand gestures," the other man said confidently. "That's what women want, big, romantic crap, like that shit people put on the Internet."

"You think?" he asked. Emily didn't seem like the grand gestures type, but he was apparently crap at knowing what she wanted while this idiot had somehow managed to move in with her after only knowing her a couple of weeks. Of course, she treated him as a cross between an irritating kid brother and a clever pet, but still, maybe Taliaferro knew what he was talking about when it came to Emily.

Michael nodded sagely.

Nick's drunken brain started to churn. He could do grand gestures. He was good at planning. Maybe, he hadn't lost yet after all. When had he ever given up on a deal? A plan started to form in his head and his grin widened

Finding Love in the Sweet Life

"This is amazing," Moira Walters, one of the hosts of Philly Mornings gushed. "I can't believe it's completely gluten free."

Nick hated mornings, and doing a live, chirpy morning show was low on his wish list, but they'd had to make nice after Taliaferro's black eye had caused them to miss the taping of the weekly magazine Moira also hosted.

The spot actually seemed to be going pretty well. Emily and Robin had done a cooking demonstration with Moira's co-host and he was fielding questions. So he played nice, nodded and smiled conspiratorially at her.

"That's why we knew we had to get the ladies behind Sweet Life to do a product line for us," he said in a confiding tone. "We're so excited for people to try all of the Guilt Free Indulgence products. You can already get a gluten-free apple muffin kit on our website as part of our exclusive preview and the full line will be hitting the stores along with the website later this year."

"And we can't wait," Moira said. "But, I think more has been cooking at Indulgence than muffins.

There's been a lot of gossip about another one of your chefs."

"That's true," Nick agreed. "Michael Taliaferro does make life interesting and I think he's doing your show next week."

She laughed. "He is, and that should be an exciting one, but from what I hear, there has been even more going on behind the scenes at Indulgence than we've heard." Moira was more chipper than usual today, a frightening prospect, because he'd let her in on the romantic gesture he'd spent the last few days planning. She was so enthusiastic about it; she was almost bouncing in her chair.

He probably should be nervous, but this felt right. He was moving fast, but as soon as he'd thought of it, he'd known it was the way to go. Emily was worried he couldn't commit to her and didn't want to take their relationship public and this would show her he was a hundred percent committed. She was it for him and he'd known it pretty much from the moment he'd met her. He'd handled the whole relationship/ work balance badly, he admitted, but this would make up for it.

"There has," he agreed. "It's definitely not what I expected when we brought Emily and Robin on, but I couldn't be happier."

Emily felt like she was having an out of body experience when she heard Moira call her over to the main set from her post in the studio's kitchen. She had to keep repeating, "Live TV, live TV," in her head to keep a smile on her face and to keep herself from bolting.

She willed herself to wake up from whatever weird dream she was having, but it wasn't working. Soon enough, she was standing on the set, the center of attention. Everyone shifted and stopped what they were doing. Moira was beaming at her, and Nick was taking her hand.

"Live, TV, live TV," she repeated silently. She knew she looked like a deer in headlights as Nick knelt in front of her. Oh God, he was going to propose to her on live television. She'd broken up with him and he was going to put her on the spot in front of everyone in the area with a TV and everyone in the world with access to YouTube. She thought she might vomit.

"Emily, I know this is fast, but I can't imagine my life without you. I knew the minute I saw you that this is what I wanted. Will you marry me?" He was holding out a velvet box with a frighteningly large diamond ring in it.

She heard a whimper and realized it had come from her own throat. "Live, TV, live TV," she repeated in her head and forced herself to say, "yes." It sounded garbled and strange, but maybe, everyone would expect that.

As soon as the word left her mouth, Nick slid the ring on her finger. He'd gotten the size right at least, she thought a little hysterically. Then, he was hugging her, and she was crying. He kissed her, and she forced herself to let him even though she wanted to punch him.

Feeling like she was going to throw up, she accepted congratulations from Moira, her co-host and a few others as soon as they went to commercial. Nick's arm around her shoulders felt heavy and confining.

"I think she needs a minute," Robin said smiling brightly. She tugged Emily's arm. Nick started to protest, but something in Robin's look must have stopped him, so he just nodded, kissed her on the cheek and let her go with Robin.

Something was wrong. Nick could feel it. At first, he'd thought everything had gone perfectly. Emily had certainly looked surprised and overwhelmed, but then, something close to panic had overtaken her features. He told himself he was being ridiculous. It had just been a lot to take in. All of the women on set were raving about how romantic it had been, he assured himself. He'd feel better, though, if he could hear it from her. The problem was he couldn't find her.

Once he'd extricated himself from all of people in the studio who wanted to offer congratulations, he'd gone in search of Emily, but no one had seen her. He tried not to panic.

"Mr. Hawkins," one of the production assistants called.

He forced a smile. "Yes?"

"Your fiancé asked me to tell you she would see you at your apartment."

"Thanks," he said, relieved. Emily had probably just wanted to get out of the studio. He smiled. He had the rest of the day off, and he had plans. Michael Taliaferro, as it turned out, was a genius.

Nick was a freaking idiot. She couldn't believe he'd done this to her. He knew she hadn't even wanted to appear in stupid cooking videos, so how could he think she'd want to have to answer a proposal on live television? She hated having people stare at her, and he'd forced her to be the center of attention.

She paced his living room too keyed up to sit down. He'd be here any minute. She forced herself to take slow, deep breaths. She needed to handle this quickly and decisively and not freak out. She ran a hand over her face and hissed as the terrifying ring scraped her skin. She pulled it off and sat it on the coffee table as if it were a poisonous snake. It glittered hatefully as it caught the sunlight spilling through the large windows.

Where was he? She needed to get this over with and get home. Robin was waiting for her in a coffee shop down the block. She'd wanted to take Emily home right away, but Emily had insisted she was going to Nick's to return the ring and end this lunacy as quickly as possible. She looked at the ring and considered just leaving it. He'd get the message and she could crawl into her bed and get a head start on avoiding the million phone calls that were going to come pouring in after that stunt he'd just pulled on live television.

She thought about leaving the country. Maybe, there were still places in the world you could start over with a new name. Finding one of them would probably be easier than untangling the mess Nick had caused today. Oh God, she was going to have to tell her parents she'd broken another engagement.

Before she could decide in favor of fleeing the apartment and maybe the country, she heard the door and whirled to face Nick. He was grinning sappily at her. A few weeks ago, that look would have made her melt. Today, she wanted to punch him in his all too handsome face.

"Emily," he said and held out his arms.

She blinked at him. How could she have been in love with someone this stupid?

His goofy, satisfied grin drooped around the edges. "What?" he asked, sounding uncertain.

Diann Dean

"Have you completely lost your damn mind?"

Chapter 25

Nick blinked at Emily. She was pissed and she wasn't wearing her ring. He looked away from her to see it sitting on the coffee table. He swallowed hard, and all of his misgivings came flooding back. He shook his head. "I don't understand."

She opened her mouth, seemed to think better of whatever she'd been going to say and snapped it shut again. After a long, deep breath, she said, "You proposed to me on live TV. I told you I didn't think this relationship would work and then you asked me to marry you in a situation where I pretty much couldn't say no."

"I thought you wanted a commitment," he said. "I thought it would be romantic." He sat down heavily in one of his leather chairs. Normally he'd have stood until she sat, but she was pacing and seemed full of angry energy, and he just felt gutted.

"Romantic?" She shook her head as if to clear it. "Nick, I didn't want an instant commitment. I didn't want you to jump into marriage. All I wanted was not to have to keep our dating some kind of state secret at Indulgence and not to have every conversation be a minefield where we had to avoid some complicated list of topics." She paused and then said bitterly, "I wanted you to care more about me than about 'optics'."

He flinched. That had been a poor choice of words. "I do Emily," he assured her. "That's what I was trying to show you."

She looked at him as if he were insane. "Nick, my mother doesn't even know we were dating because you wanted to keep everything quiet. Other than the two of us, three people in the world knew we were together. You went from five people in the world to the whole world in 30 seconds."

"I thought it would be a grand gesture," he said. "I want to commit and I wanted everyone to know it. I wanted you to know it."

He saw some of her anger deflate. Her eyes were full of unshed tears, and she looked sad and a little lost. "You want to win Nick," she said gently. "I get it. I said no and you don't take no for an answer. You up'd your game and that meant proposals on television and a giant diamond ring, but I'm not that girl." She blinked back her tears. "You know I don't like having decisions made for me, being backed into corners and you put me in a position where I couldn't say no."

"I'm sorry Em," he said, and he was hurt, and he was angry at her, at himself, at the world in general. "I just wanted to make you happy."

She made a choked sound. "God Nick. You asked me to marry you, and you've never even told me you love me."

He started to protest, but then, he realized she was right. Before he could tell her that of course he loved her, she held up a hand.

"Don't," she pleaded. "I can't hear it right now, not like this. I just can't right now."

Over his protests, she left and he sat stunned, staring for a long while at the door through which she'd disappeared.

"It's my fault," Michael admitted.

Emily blinked at him, confused.

"What the hell are you talking about?" Mia asked. She, Emily and Robin were commiserating over ice cream three days after what Robin had dubbed Proposalpocalypse. Mia claimed that calling it that made it sound like something you needed a proctologist to deal with, but Robin insisted on the name. Emily wished they didn't have to call it anything. After three days of dealing with congratulations and comments and family phone calls, she wished she could make it never have happened.

"I kind of told Hawkins that it would be a good way to get you back," Michael said.

Emily felt a little dizzy. "You what?" she snapped at her annoying temporary roommate.

He swallowed and paced over to the unoccupied chair. After he flopped down, he gave her his patented puppy look. She was unmoved.

"What did you do, moron?" Mia asked.

Michael shot her a glare, and then looked at Emily contritely. "We got drunk together, Hawkins and me. You remember that night he came here and told us about the leaks and you kicked him to the curb?"

Emily nodded impatiently. She wondered if smacking him on the head would get the story out any faster. It might at least make her feel better.

"Yeah, well anyway, he looked like he needed a drink or ten that night, so I took him to a bar." He shrugged. "He looked like he needed it and I kind of felt sorry for the bastard."

"Okay, so you guys got drunk in a bar. How did that end with Nick springing some insane proposal on live television?" Robin asked. She punctuated the question by jabbing her spoon in his direction.

"Yeah," he said, looking nervously from Robin to Mia to Emily. "Well, we didn't actually get drunk in the bar. We just got a little buzzed because there was this hot redhead...."

"What?" Emily asked, not liking at all where this story was going.

"No, no," he assured her. "She was totally into me. Hawkins was too messed up over you to even pay attention to the women giving him the eye, and there were a few."

Before he could continue with his bizarre story, Mia cut him off. "If you don't get to the point in the next ten seconds, I'm going to fillet you."

A challenging light appeared in his eyes, but before he could say something that would cause Mia to kill him and end Emily's chance of ever hearing the end of this story, she said, "Michael, please, just tell me what happened before this ice cream melts and I start crying."

He nodded, and his face turned serious, "Sorry. After we left the bar, we went back to the city and got drunk at Hawkins' place. It's kind of fuzzy because I was freaking wasted, but I told him that if he wanted to get you back, he needed to go big or go home." As all three of them glared at him, he added defensively, "Women like that. Most of them do anyway."

"You're lucky you're pretty," Robin told him

He glared at her. "I thought it's what you wanted, you know public commitment, a big romantic show."

Emily squeezed her eyes shut. Were all men this emotionally tone deaf? "I can't believe you told him that, and I can't believe he was stupid enough to listen to you." Then, something else occurred to her and she added, "And I can't believe you waited three days to tell me."

He shrugged. "I thought you'd come around and then, I didn't want you to be pissed at me, but then, I started to feel like maybe it was my fault."

That was typical Michael logic. She sighed. "He shouldn't have done it no matter whose idea it was. He should have known how much I hate being backed into a corner." She looked down at her ice cream. The Heavenly Hash Robin had been all over half the state to track down didn't seem so comforting anymore. She wondered if anyone would be offended if she just went in her room, shut the door and slept for the next day or four.

Nick turned Emily's rejected ring over in his hand. He'd taken to doing that in the past few days as if just holding it could give him the answers he wanted. It hadn't done anything so far except make him slightly crazy.

He knew he should get out of this apartment and stop playing with the damn ring, but he didn't want to. He could force himself to go to work, but that was about it.

Nick scrubbed a hand over his eyes. They felt gritty, he should probably try to get some sleep again. He rubbed his jaw and winced. Shaving was also something he should probably add to his to-do list.

He should never have listened to Michael Taliaferro. He wasn't sure why he had in the first place except that the man had caught him when he was drunk and at an especially low point in his life. He'd just had to deal with being rejected by the woman he wanted most in the world and losing two trusted and vital employees after they'd each betrayed his trust, and he'd been vulnerable. When Taliaferro had offered a suggestion, he'd run with it because it had given him something concrete to do and because the idea of a grand gesture, of putting it all on the line had appealed to him. He'd just never actually prepared himself to lose.

He'd been an idiot. From the time he'd woken up hung over to the moment he'd seen the damn ring on the table instead of on Emily's finger where it belonged, he'd been running on adrenaline and delusions.

Maybe Emily was right. Except for losing his father young, he'd lived a pretty charmed life and had gotten too used to having his way. She'd challenged him when she'd rejected him and he'd run full out to try to win the prize he'd been denied. She was wrong when she said he didn't love her though.

He'd only known Emily a short time, but when he imagined his future, he couldn't see any part of it that wouldn't be better with her in it. That's what he'd been trying to show her with that ill-considered proposal. He really should have known better. You never cut to the deal before you did the prep work, but that's what he'd tried to do with the most important deal of his life.

There had to be a way to fix it.

He shook his head. This moping wasn't working, and he was sick of himself. He needed a shower and some real food and a new plan, a better plan.

Chapter 26

"Do you love her?" Mia Trent demanded. He had no idea how she'd even gotten into his office. He guessed she must have terrified his poor assistant into letting her pass and now, she stood across from his desk glaring at him like a modern-day Amazon warrior facing her enemy.

"How did you get in here?" he asked.

She shook her head. "I told your assistant it was an emergency about Emily and Robin," she said as if that should have been obvious. Really, Molly should have buzzed, but he supposed, given Mia's current mission, she could be forgiven for her lapse.

Mia looked at him expectantly, and when he didn't say anything, she repeated, "Do you love her?"

His first instinct was to give her some sort of dodge since, as a rule, he didn't talk about his feelings with strangers. Since his rules hadn't been working out too well for him lately, he squashed that instinct and decided to just go with the truth. "I do."

She glared at him as if trying to spot a lie. Then, she snorted in disgust. "Then, you're a moron."

He started to protest, but she was kind of scary and the look she shot him made him think that if he spoke, she might cut him up into little pieces. Deciding that discretion was the better part of valor, he shut his mouth.

"Also, you're not really good enough for her, but you're pretty and successful, and since she seems to love you too, you might be perfect for each other, I'm going to help you." She paused then added, "If you screw it up this time, you're on your own."

"Okay," he said not really sure what to make of the scary lady offering help, but she was one of Emily's best friends and right now, he wasn't exactly in a place where he could turn down help from this slightly terrifying woman.

"First, you can't tell anyone I helped you because Robin made me promise to stay out of it." Her snort showed him what she thought of that idea.

After he nodded in agreement, she continued, "Second, if you hurt her in any way again, they won't be able to find pieces of you big enough to identify."

In the end, Nick hadn't gone with Mia's suggestion in its original form. He'd learned his lesson from the morning show incident and Mia had a flamboyant streak that Emily lacked. He'd reworked her plan to suit Emily better. Mia, though, had helped him realize that the missing piece, the thing he needed to give to Emily was the one thing he never gave up for anyone: control.

Emily didn't want to be swept off her feet like a damsel in distress. She wanted to be his partner. Instead of giving her that, he'd cornered her and called it romance.

He looked at the computer screen, at what he'd done, and he swallowed hard. He wasn't sure he could go through with this. He rubbed the area just below his left collarbone where the tattoo, he'd gotten to commemorate his father, sat. He really wasn't good at giving up control. If he didn't do it, though, he might miss out on something every one of his instincts told him was special and he knew he'd regret it for the rest of his life.

Finding Love in the Sweet Life

He took a deep breath and sent the message. The rest was up to Emily.

Em woke up, looked at her clock and sighed. She was closing the bakery today, so she didn't have to be up for hours, but lately, even though she was tired, she wasn't sleeping well.

She's been dreaming about that ridiculous proposal. She still couldn't believe it. Never in her wildest dreams would she have dared to imagine Nick Hawkins proposing to her on a television show. It was like something out of a movie. Similar to when she'd left Pete, no one in her family would understand what she was thinking if she told them how angry it had made her. She hadn't even been quasi engaged for a week before her mother had started sending her wedding catalogs and nagging her about meeting Nick. She'd had to tell her the truth and her mother had been sympathetic about the proposal but hadn't really understood why they couldn't get married anyway since Emily obviously loved him.

Emily stretched, trying to get the knots out of her back. There was no point in lying here and brooding. She had some work she could do since it was pretty clear to her that she wasn't going to get anymore sleep.

She got up and went to the living room to snag her laptop before heading for the kitchen.

Armed with nuclear-strength coffee, she sat at the kitchen table and opened the computer. As always lately, her inbox was scary. As she scanned the new messages, a name caught her eye.

Nick.

She told herself to be calm. She worked for his company, so it shouldn't be a surprise that he was sending her messages. However, the title of this one didn't seem very businesslike. It read, "Open Me Please."

She thought about ignoring it because she didn't think she could take being torn up over him all over again right now. Unfortunately, she'd never be able to focus on anything else if she didn't know what he wanted, so she clicked it open. There was a link. It just said, "Watch Me." If he'd sent her a tape of that morning show proposal, she was going to kill him. She'd seen it, and it was just as appalling as she'd feared. How people could think it was romantic she had no idea since she'd looked like a deer in headlights the whole time.

She was pretty sure Nick wouldn't send her that, though. He had his faults, but despite recent evidence to the contrary, he wasn't stupid. He was sweet and funny and a lot of fun. She felt herself start to tear up and gave herself a sharp mental shake. She would get over this. He was not for her. She needed someone less complicated, someone who could love her.

She considered not watching the video, but ultimately, not knowing what was on it would drive her crazy, so she clicked the link.

Nick's face filled the screen. God, he was handsome. No matter how many times she saw him, she could never get used to how good looking he was. In a blue t-shirt with his hair slightly rumpled and a little bit of stubble showing, he looked casual and hot, and she really wished she had the willpower to close this without playing it. He was sitting in his apartment on the leather couch where they'd curled up to watch movies and make out, and he looked wistful. She bit her lip hard.

"Thanks for clicking this," he said and smiled into the camera. "I probably don't deserve it, but I'm glad you did. I just wanted you to know that you were right about a lot of things; about me needing to be in control, about me needing to win and about me taking shortcuts. But, you were wrong about me loving you. I was too mixed up to say it and I know you wouldn't believe me now if I said it in person, so I made you this video instead. I tried to keep what I felt for you separate from everything else in my life, and I failed. I tried to make decisions for both of us, and that didn't work well either. I took some of your control, and now, I'm giving it back to you."

She paused the video and swallowed past the lump in her throat. She didn't think she could do this. She told herself he was smart. He knew her and he hated losing. He was just telling her what she wanted to hear. She blinked back some tears and started the video again.

"This video is yours. It's not public right now. I don't talk about my feelings ever. It's easier for me to make big gestures like buying rings and proposing on television than just saying what I feel." His words were hesitant, and he was obviously uncomfortable, but he seemed determined too.

God help her, she was falling for it.

He continued, "So that's what I'm giving you: my feelings. You can keep them, ignore them or publish them to the world. Put this on YouTube if you want because I'd rather you do that than not at least hear me out."

He took a deep breath, "You spilled wine on me one day and I haven't been completely sane since then..." He went on to tell her how he felt about her, about how he hadn't been able to keep his mind on business because she'd been driving him crazy, about how jealous he'd been when he thought she was dating Michael and about how elated he was when they'd finally started dating.

The way he described her, the way he saw her was almost impossible to believe. If she hadn't been sure he was talking about her, she'd have thought he meant someone else, someone amazing and beautiful and mysterious. He thought she was mysterious. She shook her head in wonder.

After he talked about their relationship, he told her about his father, how it'd felt to lose him at such a young age and how it had made him want to control everything, to order the world to suit his wishes because he was scared of dying without ever making his dreams come true.

At the end, he said, "So, if you made it this far, you know that I'm kind of a mess." He gave her that sad, lost smile that turned her will to mush. "I hope you want to give me another chance, and I don't mean take the ring, though if you want it, it's yours. I mean start over and do it right this time," he paused and then, continued," But even if you don't want to try again, I'm hoping you at least understand and forgive me for not being brave enough to say all this to your face when I had the chance."

When he saw her name on the caller ID, Nick felt like a teenager afraid to talk to his first crush. He answered the phone and was pleasantly surprised that his voice didn't crack.

"Hi, Is this Nick Hawkins?" Emily asked. Her voice sounded scratchy like she'd been crying.

"Emily?" he asked, confused. She'd called his number. Who else did she think would be answering his phone?

"Oh good. I'm so glad you remembered me. It's Emily McCauley from the reception. I'm the one who doused you with red wine," she said, and then, he got it.

He felt a big, stupid grin spread over his face. "How could I forget you?" he asked.

"Yeah, it's kind of embarrassing, but I think you go the wrong idea about me." She sounded like she was trying not to laugh. "That guy who picked me up wasn't my boyfriend. He's my business partner's husband and my friend, so if that offer for a drink is still open, I'd kind of love to do it." Her voice broke a little.

"It's definitely open," he told her trying to avoid whooping with joy into the phone.

"Great," she said. "I should warn you though; I never sleep with a guy on the first date."

"Really?" he asked. "That sounds like a challenge, and I really like a challenge."

She laughed and said, "There's something else you should know."

"And what is that?" he asked, already wondering just how quickly he could get to her place.

"I'm considering the reception our first date," she said, and her voice was husky.

He bit back a groan. "That's good to know, hold that thought. I'll pick you up in 45 minutes."

She laughed. "Oh, I guess I forgot to tell you one other thing."

He swallowed hard. "Yes?"

"I'd really like to have that drink at your place, and as luck would have it..." She trailed off, and he heard a knock at the door.

Epilogue

"Sorry," Emily said as Robin held the door for them. "There was a lot of um, traffic." She and Nick were a little late for the party. They'd just moved into their new house and they were enjoying the extra space quite a bit.

"Uh huh," Robin said and gave her a look that said she didn't believe that excuse for a second. "It's fine. The birthday girl just woke up from her nap, and we weren't going to blow out the candles without Aunt Emily and Uncle Nick." She looked at the huge, wrapped box Nick was carrying. "Especially since it looks like they bought out the store."

Nick nodded and sighed dramatically. "She's going to bankrupt me spoiling your daughter."

Emily snorted. "Yeah, I had to keep him from buying everything in sight. If he'd had his way, we'd have had to rent a truck to get it all here."

After Nick put their present with the others on a table in the living room, they followed Robin back to the kitchen where everyone was gathered. It was a small party, just family and a few close friends.

From across the room, Mia waved at them and raised an eyebrow. Emily shrugged and gave a pointed look at the man next to Mia with his arm around her shoulder. Michael said the two of them were just friends, and Mia claimed to barely tolerate him, but since he'd moved to the city to open his restaurant, the two of them had been spending a lot of time together, and their body language suggested they were way more than friends. Whatever they were, as long as they were happy, she was happy for them.

Michael exchanged a look with Nick and winked dramatically at Emily. She stuck her tongue out at him. He still crashed at their place quite often. He seemed to enjoy trying to get Nick mad enough to kick him out.

She put her head on Nick's shoulder and he drew her even closer to his side as she turned her attention to the little girl holding court in the center of the room. Emmy Caroline Mead had a shock of dark hair like her mother and big blue eyes like her daddy. She also had a big piece of Emily's heart. Emily hadn't been able to believe it when Robin had told her that she was naming her daughter Emmy after her two best friends in the world, and Emily had fallen in love with her namesake the moment she'd first laid eyes on her.

She watched little Emmy smash her fist into the cake she and Robin had made for her, a pink and yellow confection that tasted as good as it looked. Luckily, considering the gleeful damage the girl had done, they'd made a small one for her to destroy and a larger one for the adults to enjoy.

One year old, Emily couldn't believe it. The time had gone so fast, but at the same time, so much had happened. She was so happy, she felt tears fill her eyes. Of course, lately, she cried at the drop of a hat.

"Hey now," Nick whispered in her ear. "There's no crying at this party."

She just shook her head and smiled up at him. They'd been together for longer than little Emmy had been alive, and this past year had been pretty amazing. They'd moved in together not long after their do-over first date, which had lasted about two days, and a few months ago, they'd settled on a house close to Robin and Sweet Life but still an easy commute to the city.

She and Robin had had to say goodbye to their old Sweet Life location. The attention and money from their Indulgence line had meant they could finally afford to move to a bigger shop in an area that suited the business better. It was incredible, but sometimes, she still got nostalgic for the old neighborhood, and she dragged Nick to Fratelli's for a slice. Now that they had a house ten minutes from her favorite pizzeria, she had a feeling that they'd be eating there even more often.

Later, when they were back home snuggled on their couch, Nick bent to kiss her. She smiled up at him in welcome, but before his lips met hers, she yawned.

She felt her cheeks heat. "Sorry, I must be more tired than I'd realized."

"That wasn't exactly the response I'd hoped for. Getting bored with me already?" he asked. "I thought that was only for old married people."

Emily grinned at him, "Yeah, and we aren't even engaged."

"And whose fault is that?" He shook his head. "I keep waiting for you to ask me, but you never do."

She laughed. "I guess you'll have to work harder to persuade me," she said.

"I'm trying, but you yawn in my face when I'm ready to do my best work. I must be losing my touch."

She smiled a little uncertainly. "Not exactly."

"So, what is it exactly?" he asked, moving back a little so he could watch her face.

She bit her bottom lip, She was pretty sure he was going to be at least as happy and scared and amazed about this as she was, but it wasn't something they'd planned. She took a deep breath, "It's actually your fault that I'm so tired."

He leaned closer and smiled. "Because I wore you out before?"

She shook her head, thought about it and then nodded, "Well, yeah, partly, and I'm still kind of sore from that kitchen counter experiment you wanted to try before the party," she shivered at the memory.

"We'll get it right one of these times," he promised.

"If we get it any more right, I won't survive it," she grumbled, and then, she realized she was stalling. "But that's not the main reason I've been tired lately and crying at commercials and going on midnight fridge raids..."

She saw the moment the real reason dawned on him and she felt relief followed by incredible joy.

"Really?" his million-dollar grin was just for her. "Pregnant? Are you sure?"

As she nodded, his hand touched her still-flat stomach as gently as he would have if she were made of glass.

"Yeah, I know we didn't plan it," she said. "But nothing's perfect I guess."

"This is," he said. "She's going to be perfect."

"Or he," she reminded him. "You know it could be a boy."

"Either way," he told her. "This is perfect. You're perfect." Then, it was his turn to tear up.

She sniffed. "Don't you dare cry Nick Hawkins. If you start crying, I'm going to cry and I don't want to cry.

He smiled at her. "You know what this means, though right? You're going to have to propose now since you have me in a compromising position."

"And what if I wanted to skip the proposal, you know, since we kind of suck at them and get right to the good part."

He thought about it. "I can work with that," he said as he reached for her and added against her lips, "But you're buying me a ring."

After that, there wasn't any talking, and there definitely wasn't any yawning.

Please visit www.DiannDean.com to learn more and to be the first to know about her next romance novels.

Made in the USA
Lexington, KY
03 November 2015